Gertrude Chandler Warner's

THE BOXCAR CHILDREN

GRAPHIC NOVELS

BOOK SIXTEEN

HOUSEBOAT MYSTERY

Henry, Jessie, Violet, and Benny Alden are spending a week on a houseboat! Throughout the journey, the children have the feeling they are being watched—and they are. Someone wants something on their boat, and he'll stop at nothing to get it. Can the Boxcar Children figure out who is out there before its too late?

THE BOXCAR CHILDREN
GRAPHIC NOVELS

1. THE BOXCAR CHILDREN
2. SURPRISE ISLAND
3. THE YELLOW HOUSE MYSTERY
4. MYSTERY RANCH
5. MIKE'S MYSTERY
6. BLUE BAY MYSTERY
7. SNOWBOUND MYSTERY
8. TREE HOUSE MYSTERY
9. THE HAUNTED CABIN MYSTERY
10. THE AMUSEMENT PARK MYSTERY
11. THE PIZZA MYSTERY
12. THE CASTLE MYSTERY
13. THE WOODSHED MYSTERY
14. THE LIGHTHOUSE MYSTERY
15. MOUNTAIN TOP MYSTERY
16. HOUSEBOAT MYSTERY
17. BICYCLE MYSTERY
18. MYSTERY IN THE SAND

Gertrude Chandler Warner's

THE BOXCAR CHILDREN
HOUSEBOAT MYSTERY

Adapted by Joeming Dunn
Illustrated by Ben Dunn

Henry Alden

Watch

Jessie Alden

Violet Alden

Benny Alden

magic
wagon

visit us at www.abdopublishing.com

Published by Magic Wagon, a division of the ABDO Group, 8000 West 78th Street, Edina, Minnesota 55439. Copyright © 2011 by Abdo Consulting Group, Inc. International copyrights reserved in all countries. All rights reserved. No part of this book may be reproduced in any form without written permission from the publisher.

Graphic Planet™ is a trademark and logo of Magic Wagon.

This edition produced by arrangement with Albert Whitman & Company. THE BOXCAR CHILDREN is a registered trademark of Albert Whitman & Company. www.albertwhitman.com

Printed in the United States of America, North Mankato, Minnesota.
092010
012011

This book contains 10% recycled materials.

Adapted by Joeming Dunn
Illustrated by Ben Dunn
Colored by Robby Bevard
Lettered by Doug Dlin
Edited by Stephanie Hedlund
Interior layout and design by Kristen Fitzner Denton
Cover art by Ben Dunn
Book design and packaging by Shannon Eric Denton

Library of Congress Cataloging-in-Publication Data

Dunn, Joeming W.
 Houseboat mystery / adapted by Joeming Dunn ; illustrated by Ben Dunn.
     p. cm. -- (Boxcar children graphic novels)
 At head of title: Gertrude Chandler Warner's The Boxcar children.
 "Graphic Planet"--Copyright p.
 ISBN 978-1-61641-124-4
 1. Graphic novels. [1. Graphic novels. 2. Mystery and detective stories. 3. Houseboats--Fiction. 4. Brothers and sisters--Fiction. 5. Orphans--Fiction. 6. Warner, Gertrude Chandler, 1890-1979. Houseboat mystery--Adaptations.] I. Dunn, Ben, ill. II. Warner, Gertrude Chandler, 1890-1979. Houseboat mystery. III. Title.
 PZ7.7.D86Ho 2011
 741.5'973--dc22

                                            2010016151

BOOK SIXTEEN
HOUSEBOAT MYSTERY

Contents

Houseboat for Rent 6
Trouble Brewing 11
The Auction 16
Something's Wrong! 23
A Discovery 25
Trapped! 28

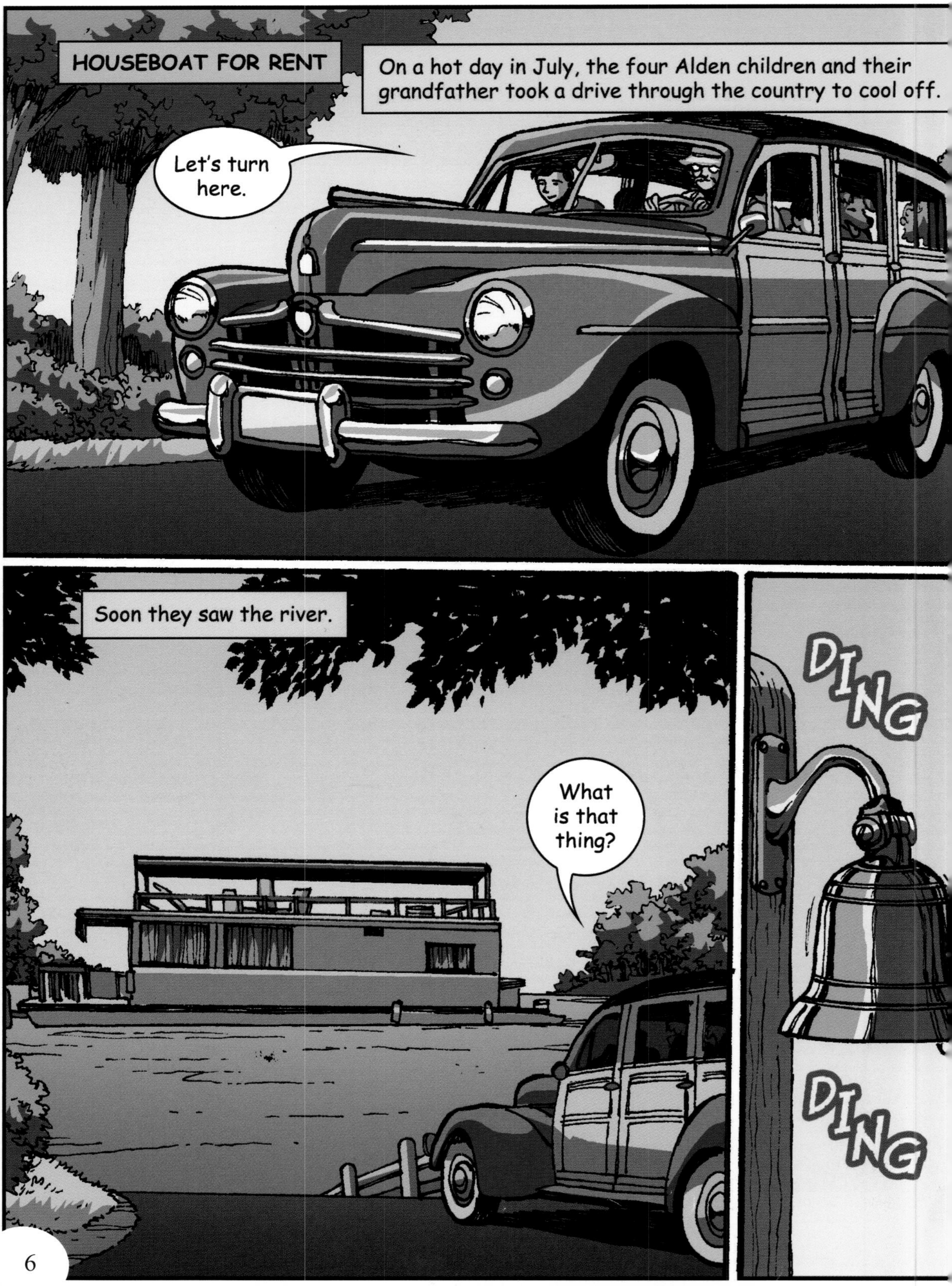
HOUSEBOAT FOR RENT
On a hot day in July, the four Alden children and their grandfather took a drive through the country to cool off.
Let's turn here.
Soon they saw the river.
What is that thing?
DING
DING

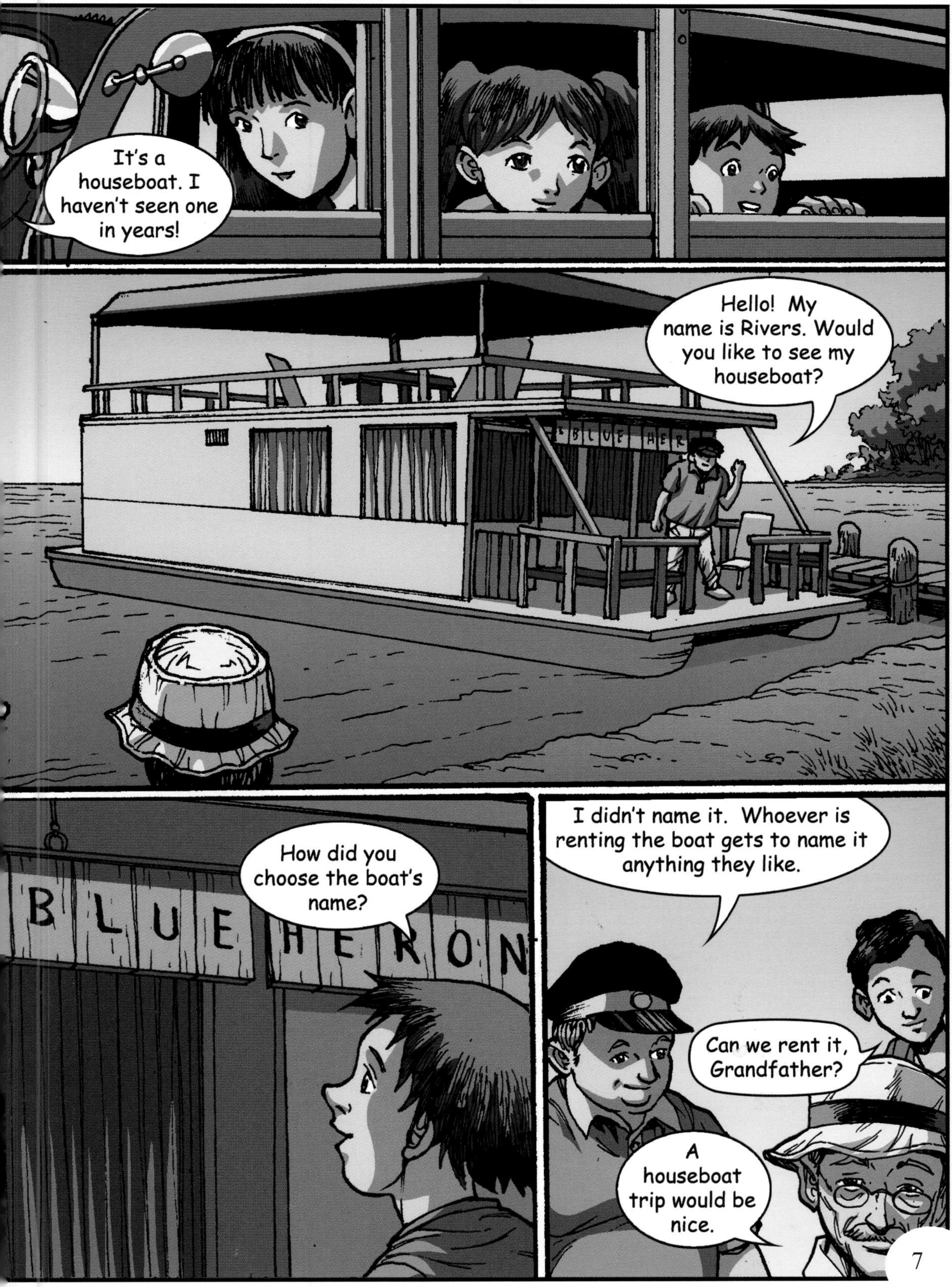
It's a houseboat. I haven't seen one in years!
Hello! My name is Rivers. Would you like to see my houseboat?
BLUE HER
BLUE HERON
How did you choose the boat's name?
I didn't name it. Whoever is renting the boat gets to name it anything they like.
Can we rent it, Grandfather?
A houseboat trip would be nice.

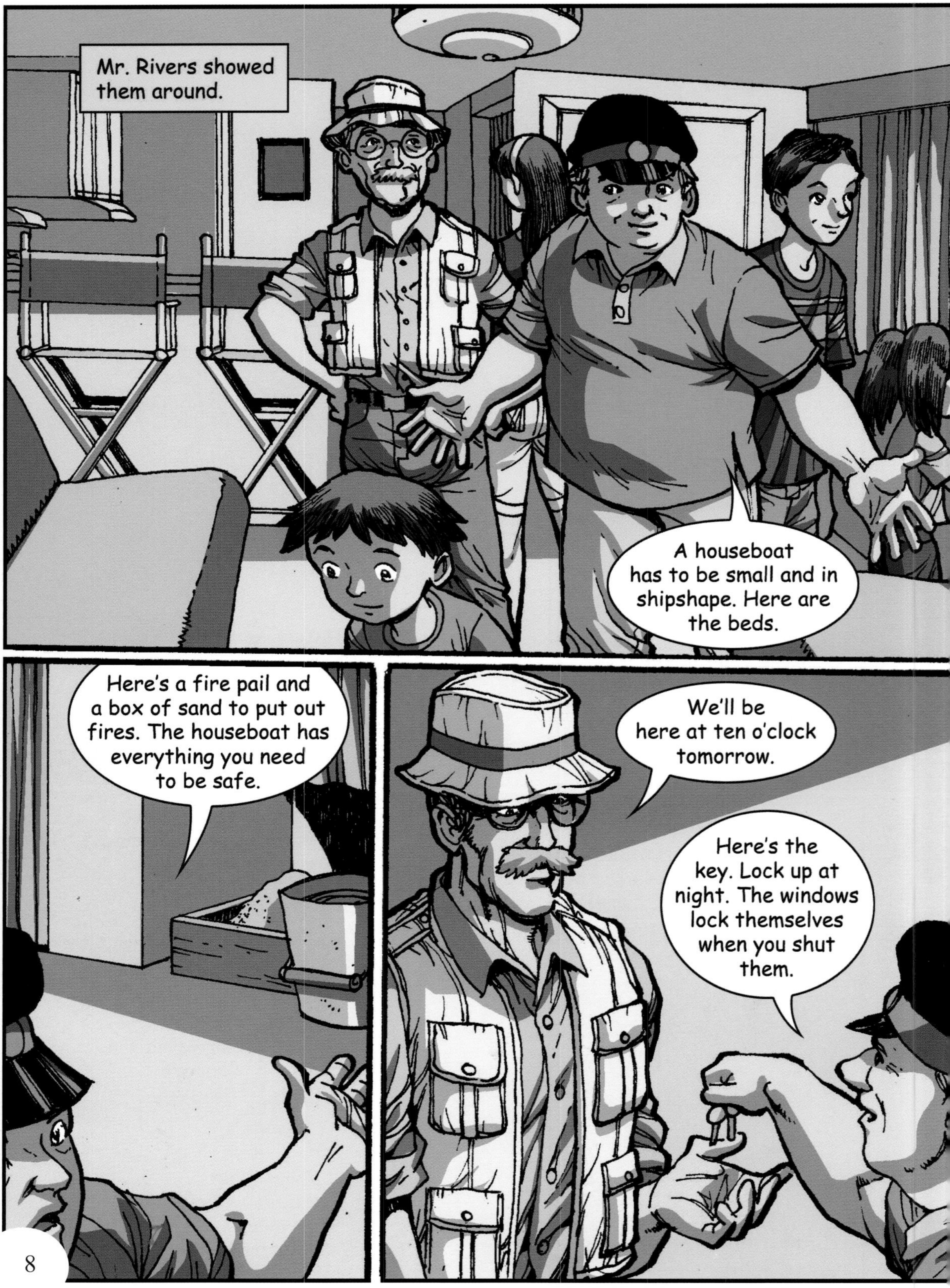
Mr. Rivers showed them around.
A houseboat has to be small and in shipshape. Here are the beds.
Here's a fire pail and a box of sand to put out fires. The houseboat has everything you need to be safe.
We'll be here at ten o'clock tomorrow.
Here's the key. Lock up at night. The windows lock themselves when you shut them.

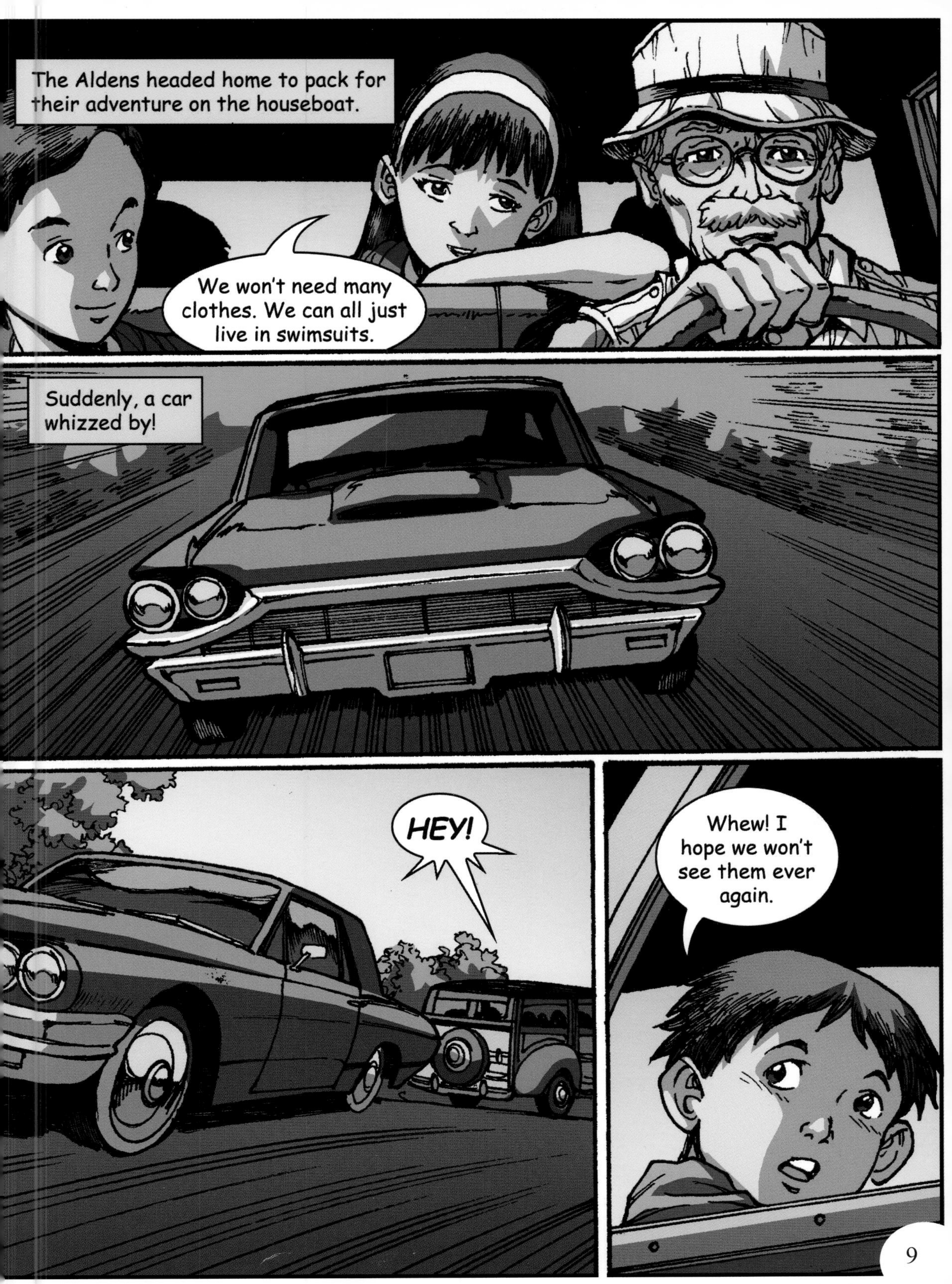
The Aldens headed home to pack for their adventure on the houseboat.
We won't need many clothes. We can all just live in swimsuits.
Suddenly, a car whizzed by!
HEY!
Whew! I hope we won't see them ever again.

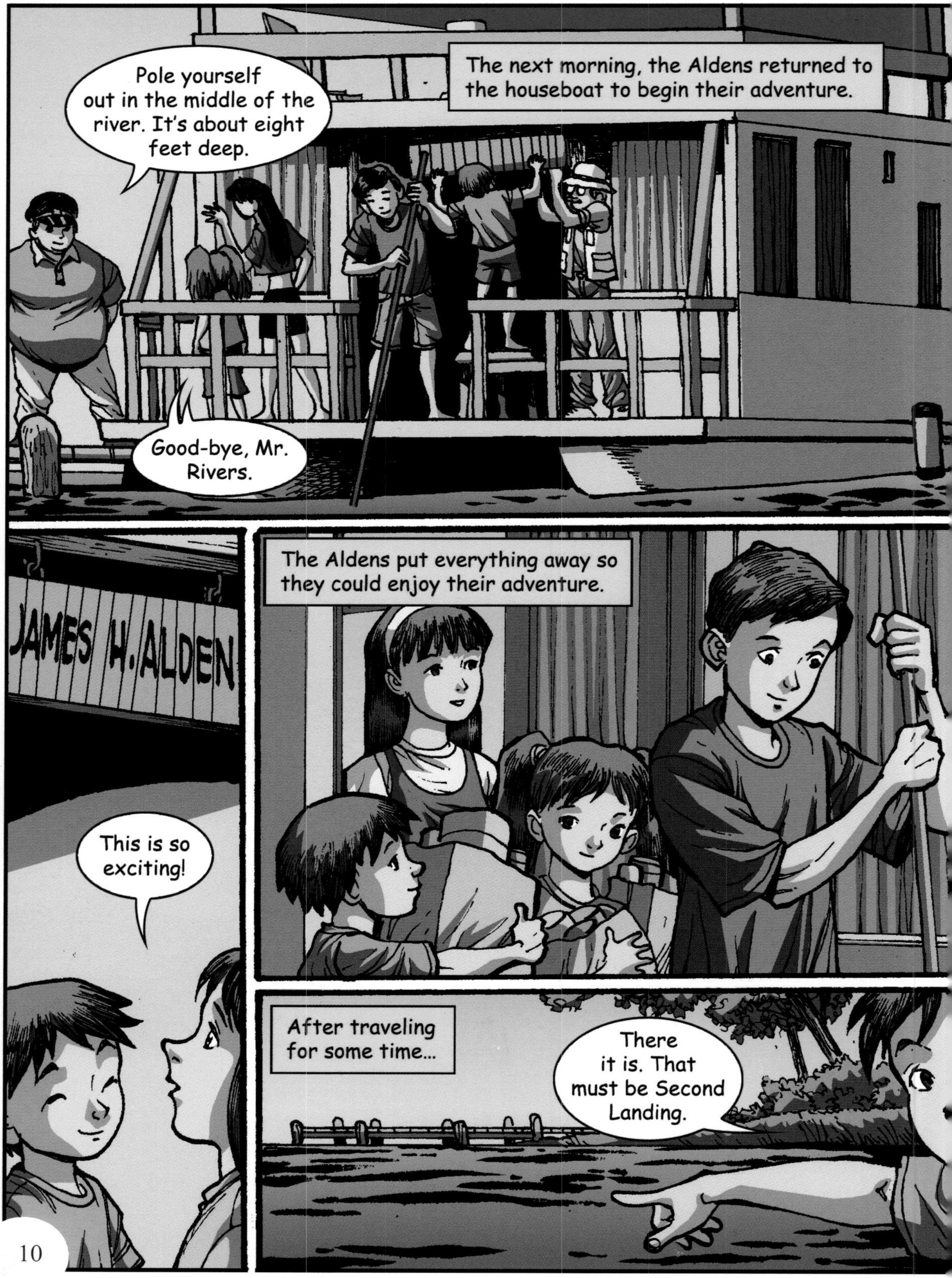
The next morning, the Aldens returned to the houseboat to begin their adventure.
Pole yourself out in the middle of the river. It's about eight feet deep.
Good-bye, Mr. Rivers.
JAMES H. ALDEN
This is so exciting!
The Aldens put everything away so they could enjoy their adventure.
After traveling for some time...
There it is. That must be Second Landing.

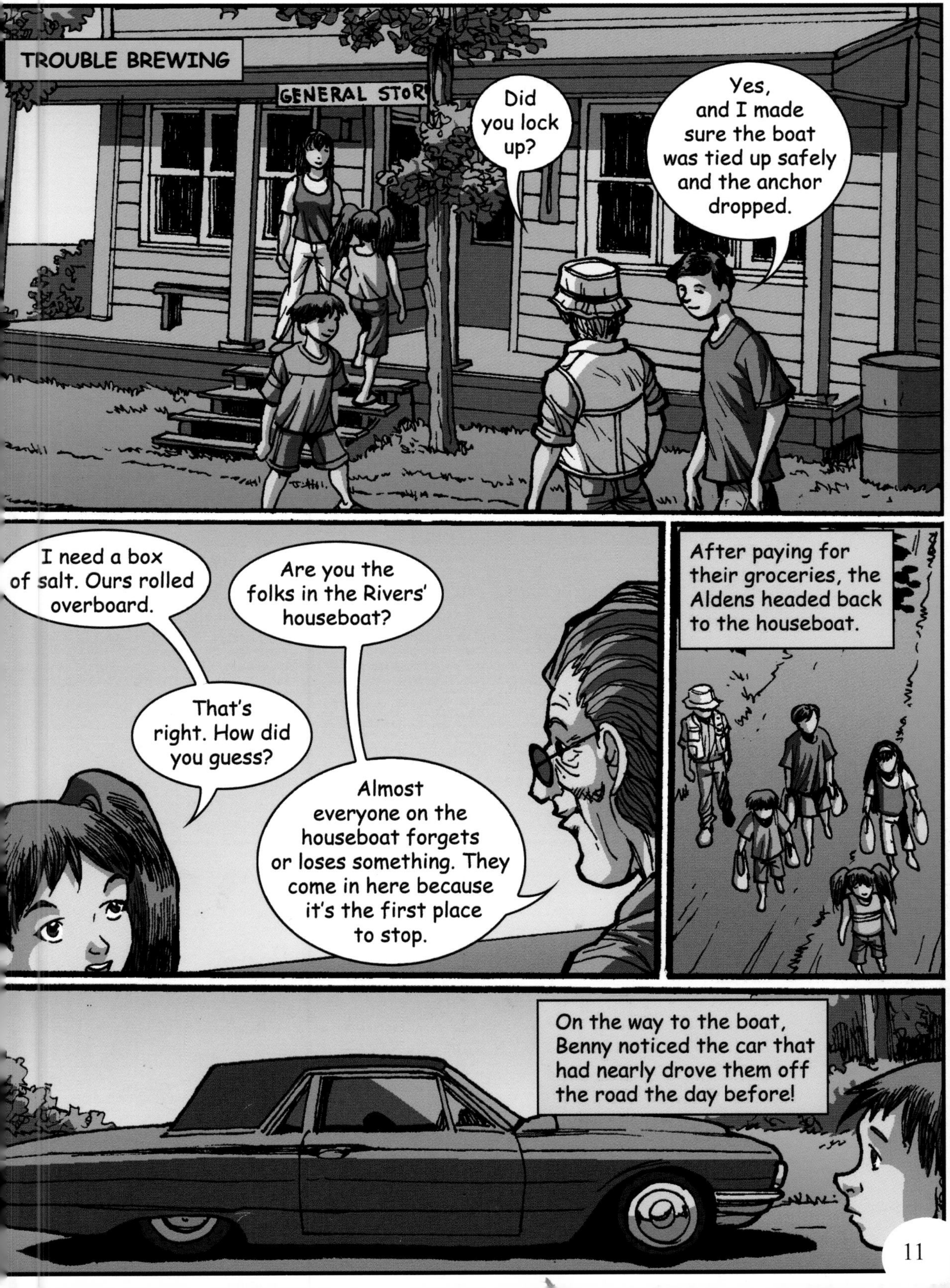
TROUBLE BREWING
GENERAL STOR
Did you lock up?
Yes, and I made sure the boat was tied up safely and the anchor dropped.
I need a box of salt. Ours rolled overboard.
Are you the folks in the Rivers' houseboat?
That's right. How did you guess?
Almost everyone on the houseboat forgets or loses something. They come in here because it's the first place to stop.
After paying for their groceries, the Aldens headed back to the houseboat.
On the way to the boat, Benny noticed the car that had nearly drove them off the road the day before!

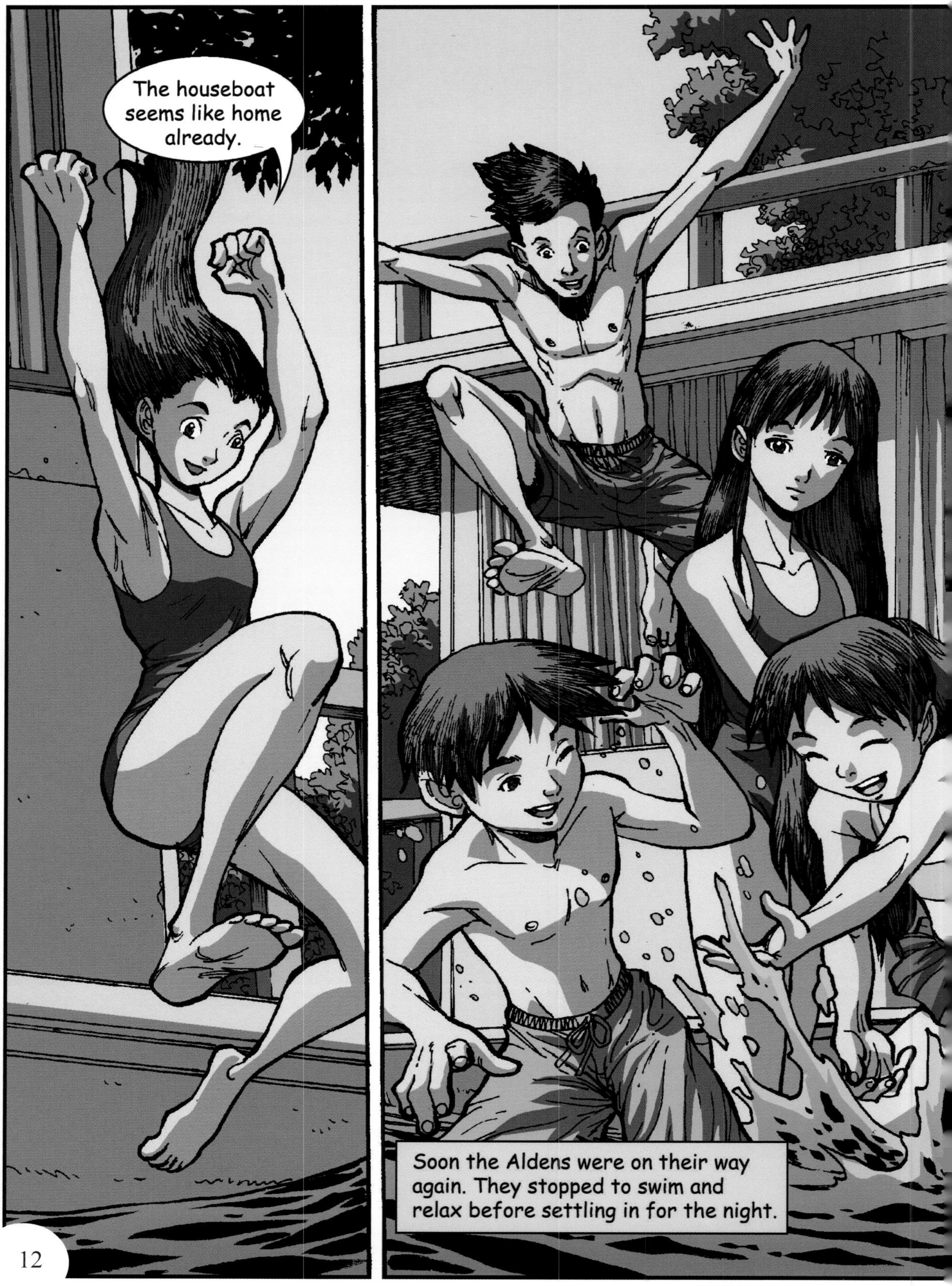

The houseboat seems like home already.
Soon the Aldens were on their way again. They stopped to swim and relax before settling in for the night.

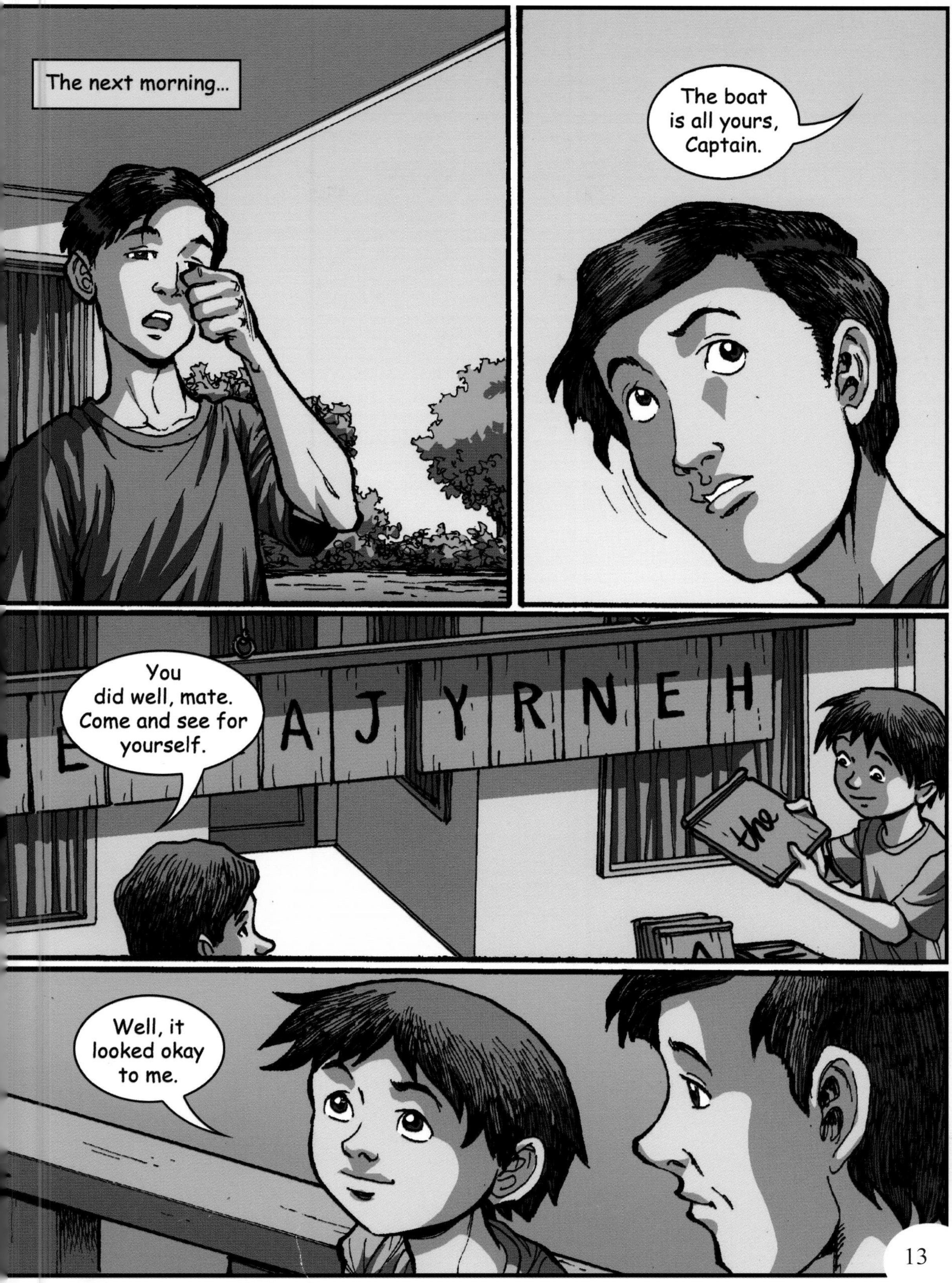
The next morning...
The boat is all yours, Captain.
AJYRNEH
You did well, mate. Come and see for yourself.
the
Well, it looked okay to me.

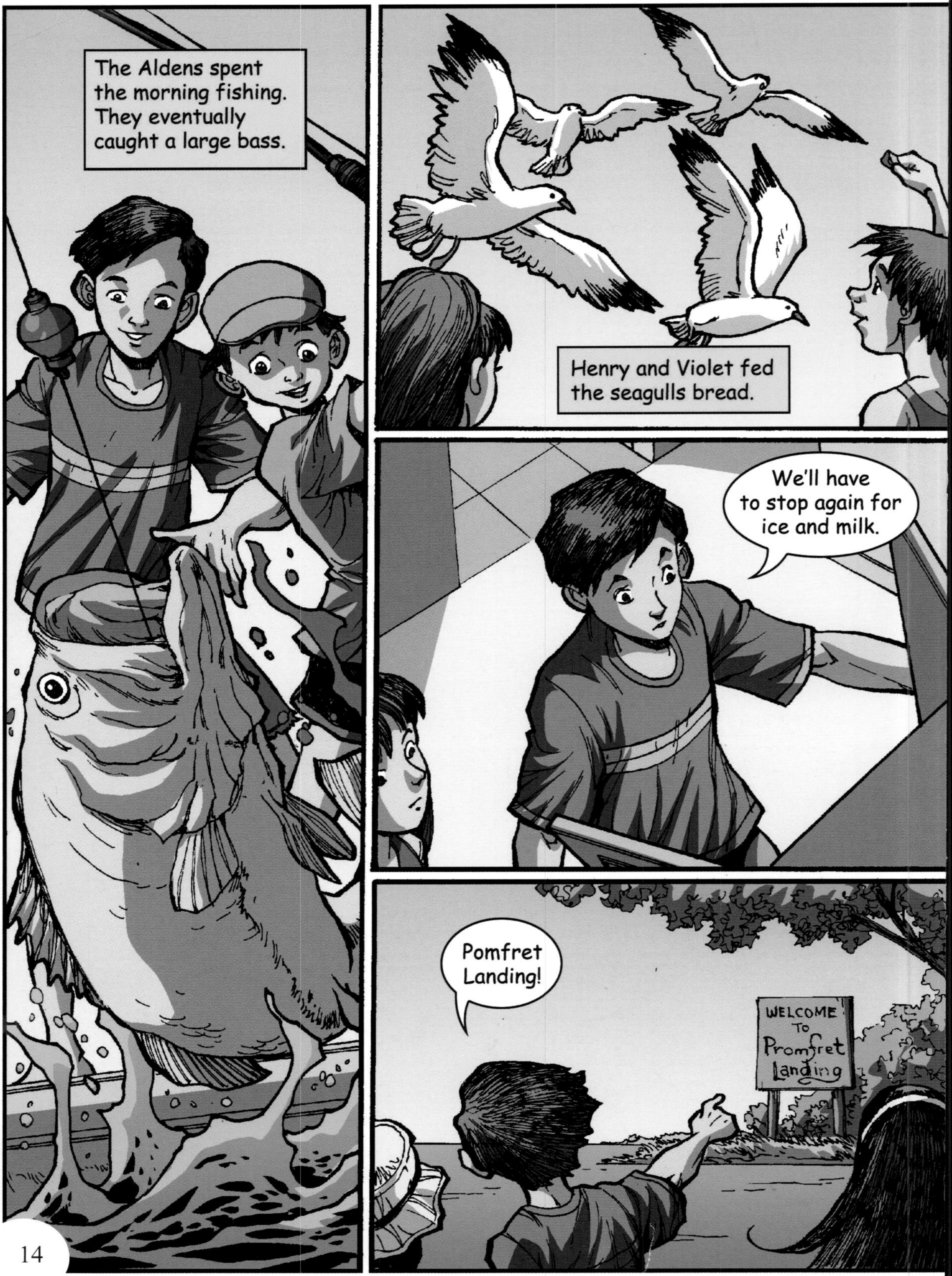
The Aldens spent the morning fishing. They eventually caught a large bass.
Henry and Violet fed the seagulls bread.
We'll have to stop again for ice and milk.
Pomfret Landing!
WELCOME TO Promfret Landing

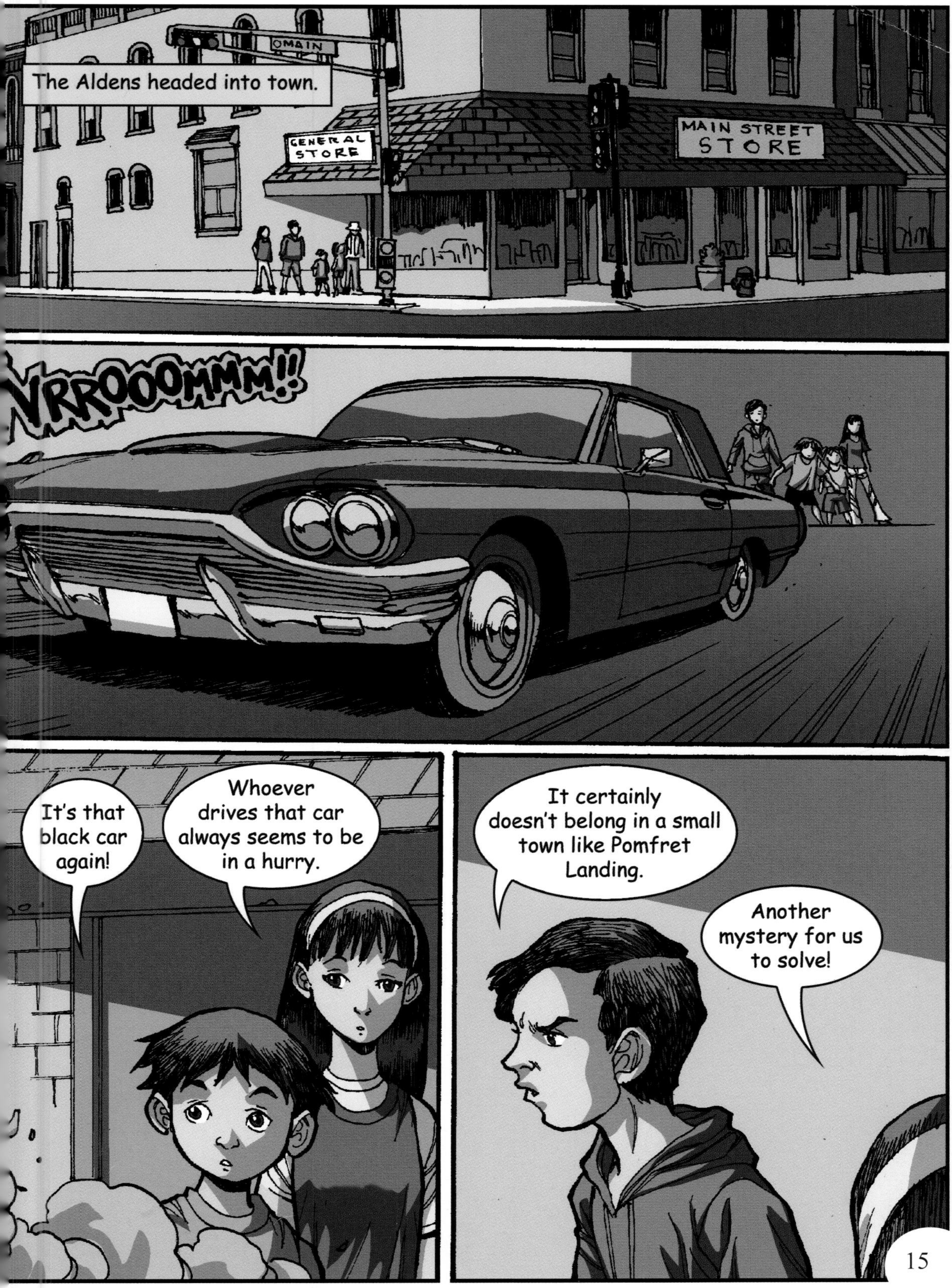
MAIN
The Aldens headed into town.
GENERAL STORE
MAIN STREET STORE
VRROOOMMM!!
It's that black car again!
Whoever drives that car always seems to be in a hurry.
It certainly doesn't belong in a small town like Pomfret Landing.
Another mystery for us to solve!

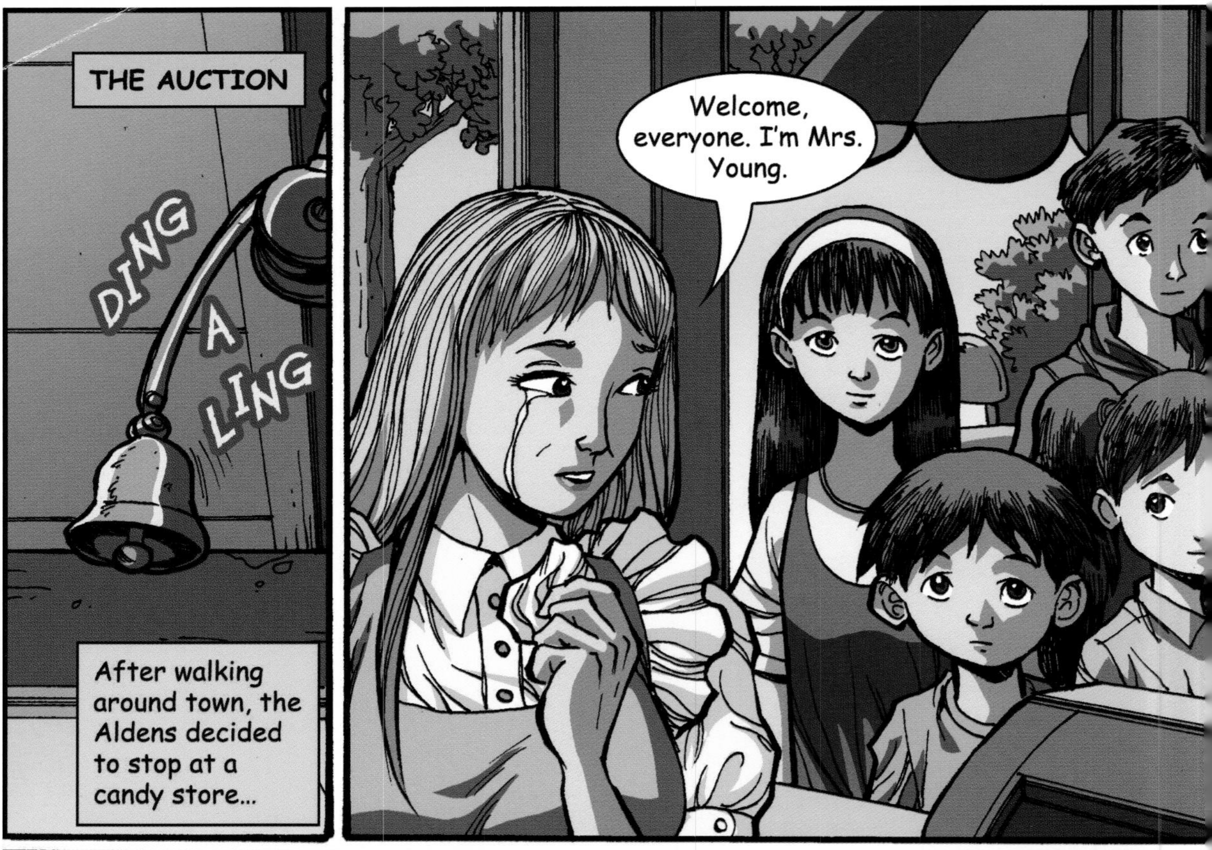
THE AUCTION
DING A LING
After walking around town, the Aldens decided to stop at a candy store...
Welcome, everyone. I'm Mrs. Young.

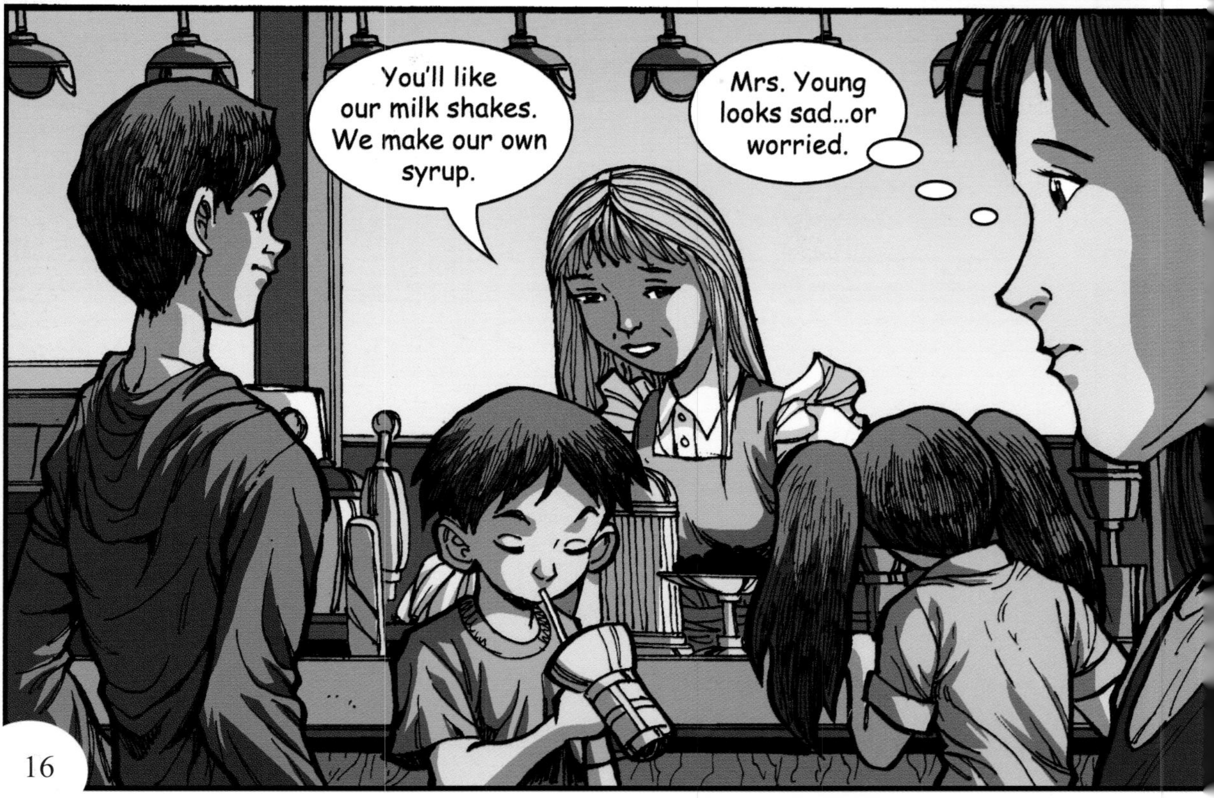
You'll like our milk shakes. We make our own syrup.
Mrs. Young looks sad...or worried.

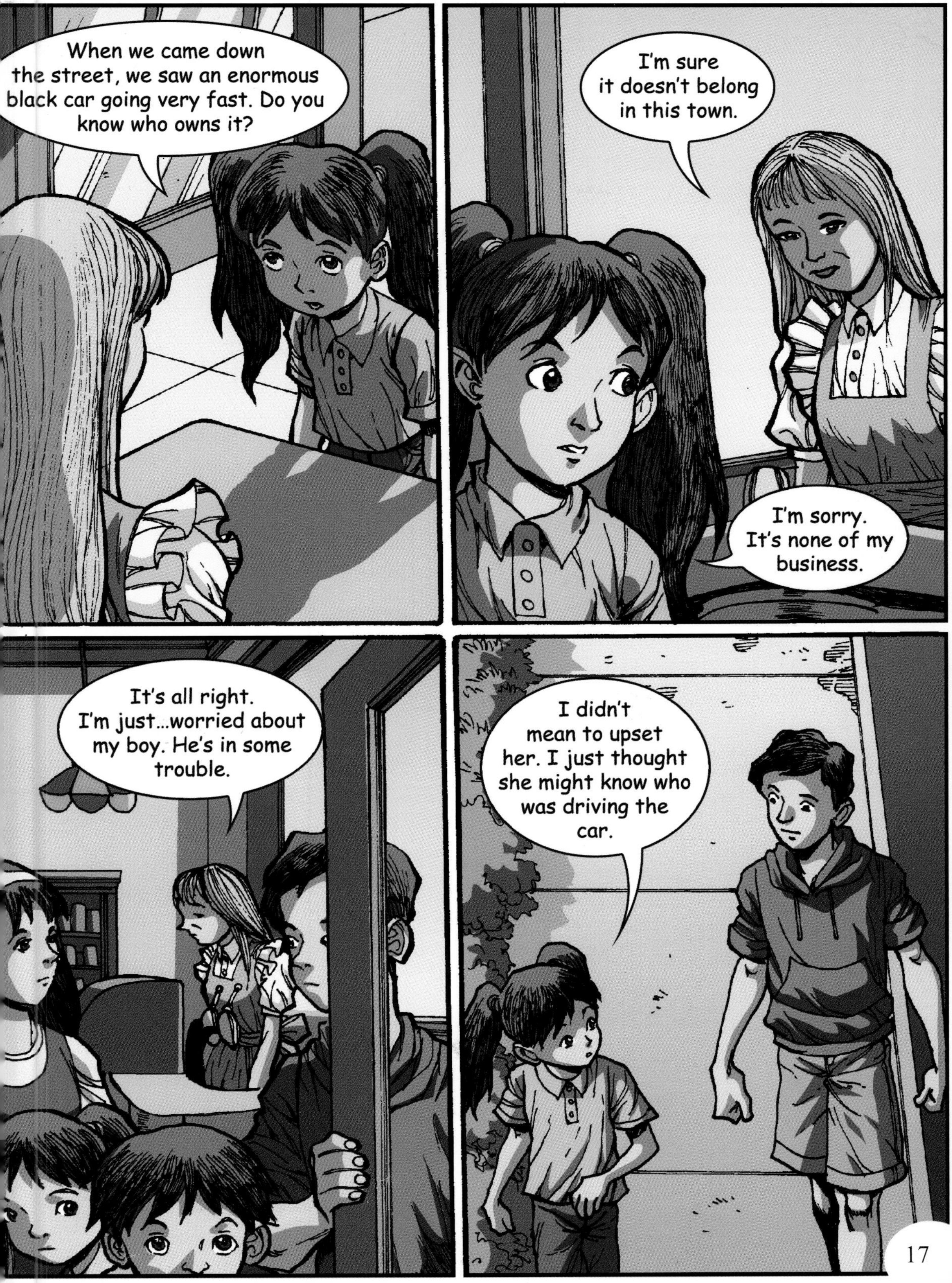
When we came down the street, we saw an enormous black car going very fast. Do you know who owns it?
I'm sure it doesn't belong in this town.
I'm sorry. It's none of my business.
It's all right. I'm just...worried about my boy. He's in some trouble.
I didn't mean to upset her. I just thought she might know who was driving the car.

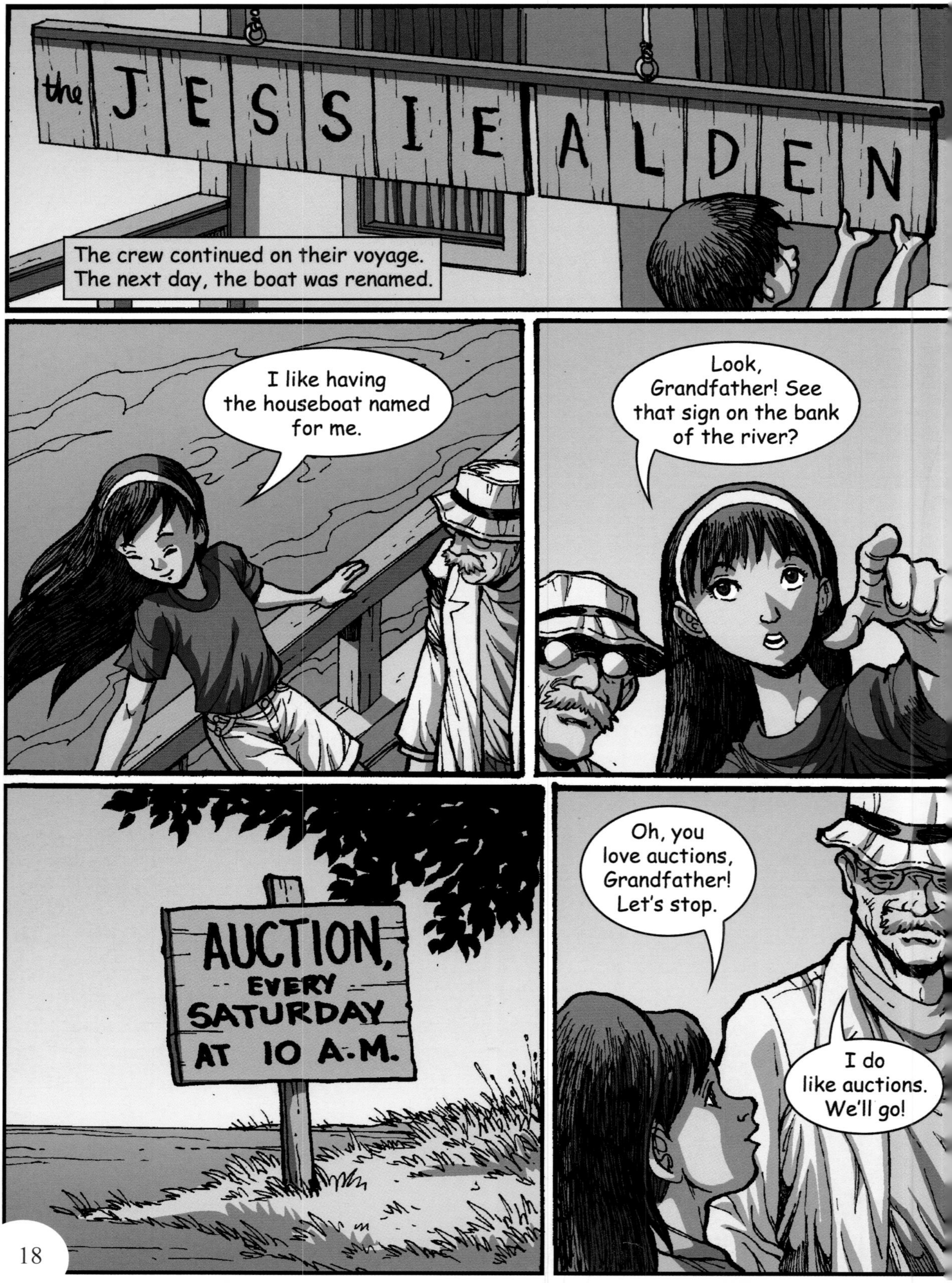
the JESSIE ALDEN
The crew continued on their voyage. The next day, the boat was renamed.
I like having the houseboat named for me.
Look, Grandfather! See that sign on the bank of the river?
AUCTION, EVERY SATURDAY AT 10 A.M.
Oh, you love auctions, Grandfather! Let's stop.
I do like auctions. We'll go!

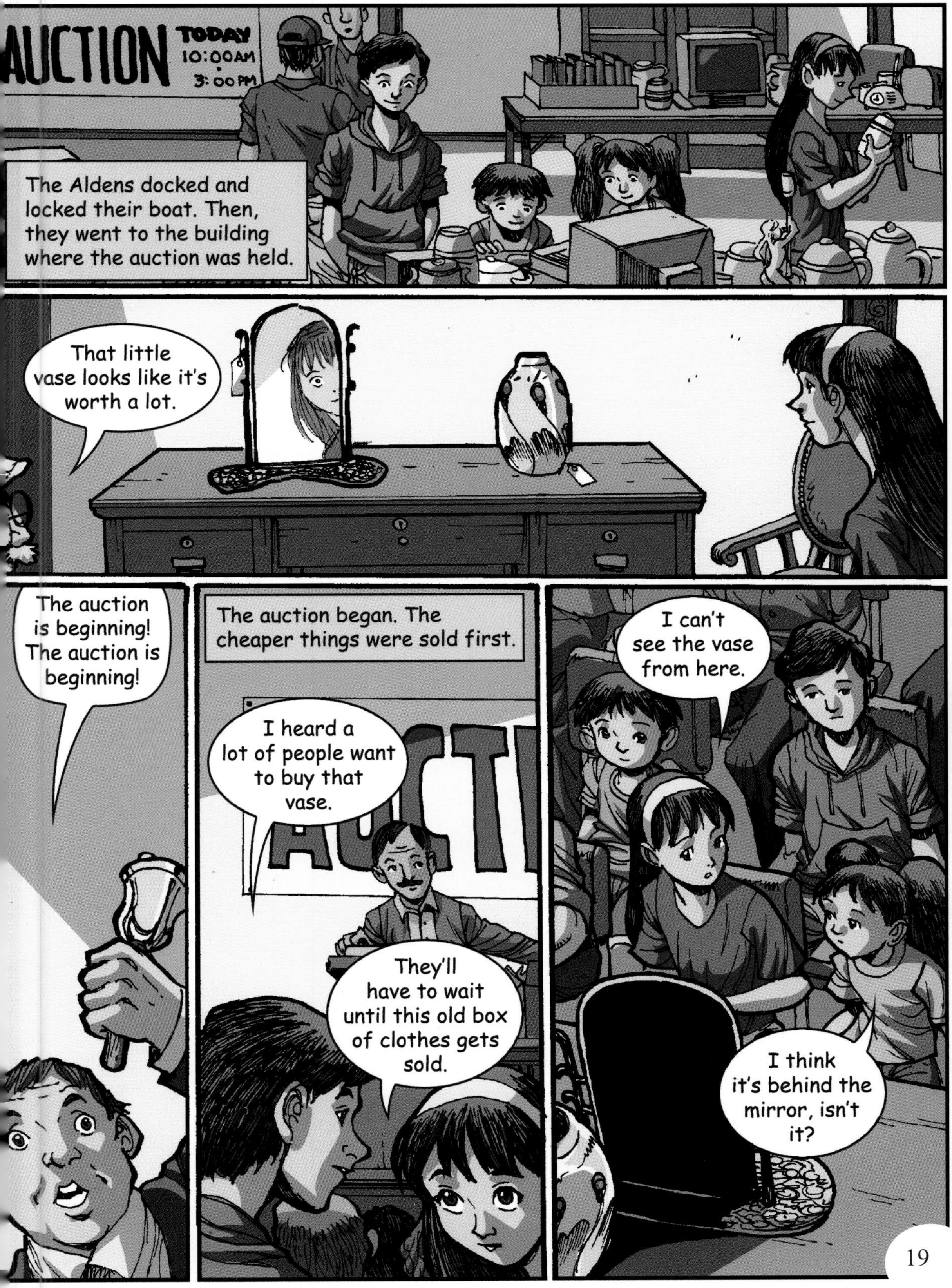
AUCTION TODAY 10:00AM 3:00PM
The Aldens docked and locked their boat. Then, they went to the building where the auction was held.
That little vase looks like it's worth a lot.
The auction is beginning! The auction is beginning!
The auction began. The cheaper things were sold first.
I heard a lot of people want to buy that vase.
They'll have to wait until this old box of clothes gets sold.
I can't see the vase from here.
I think it's behind the mirror, isn't it?

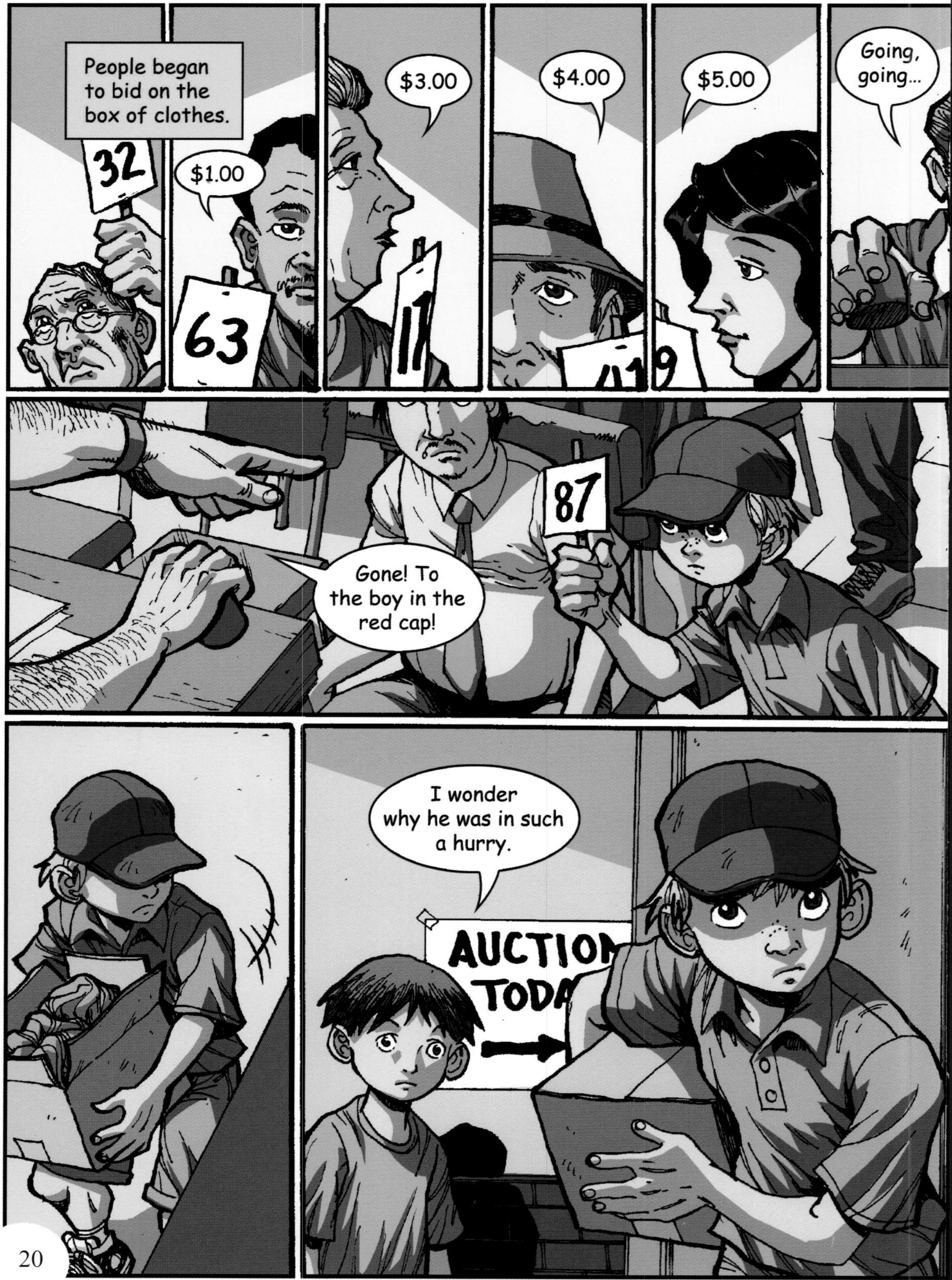

People began to bid on the box of clothes.
32
$1.00
63
$3.00
17
$4.00
$5.00
419
Going, going...
87
Gone! To the boy in the red cap!
I wonder why he was in such a hurry.
AUCTION TODA

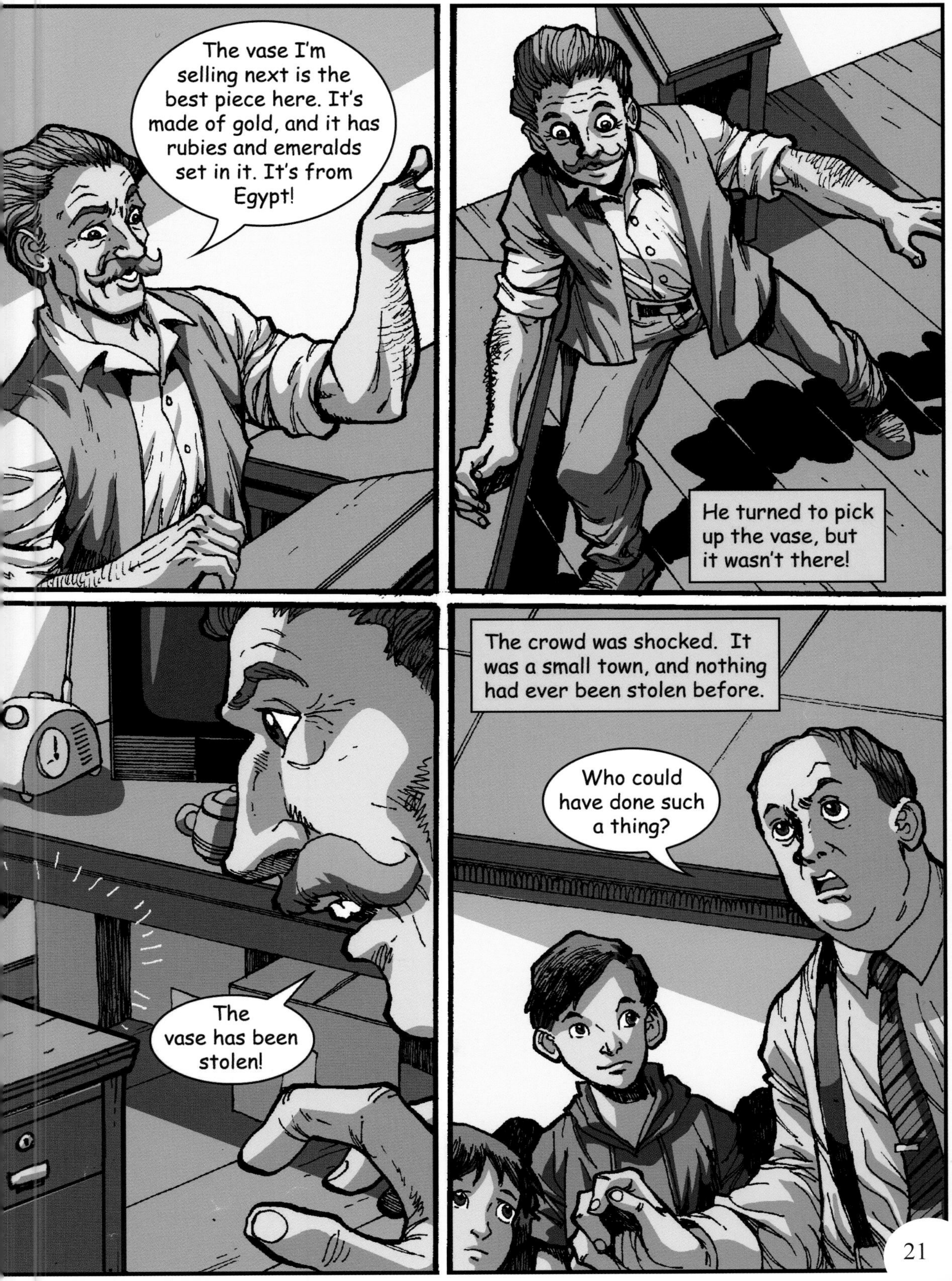

The vase I'm selling next is the best piece here. It's made of gold, and it has rubies and emeralds set in it. It's from Egypt!
He turned to pick up the vase, but it wasn't there!
The vase has been stolen!
The crowd was shocked. It was a small town, and nothing had ever been stolen before.
Who could have done such a thing?

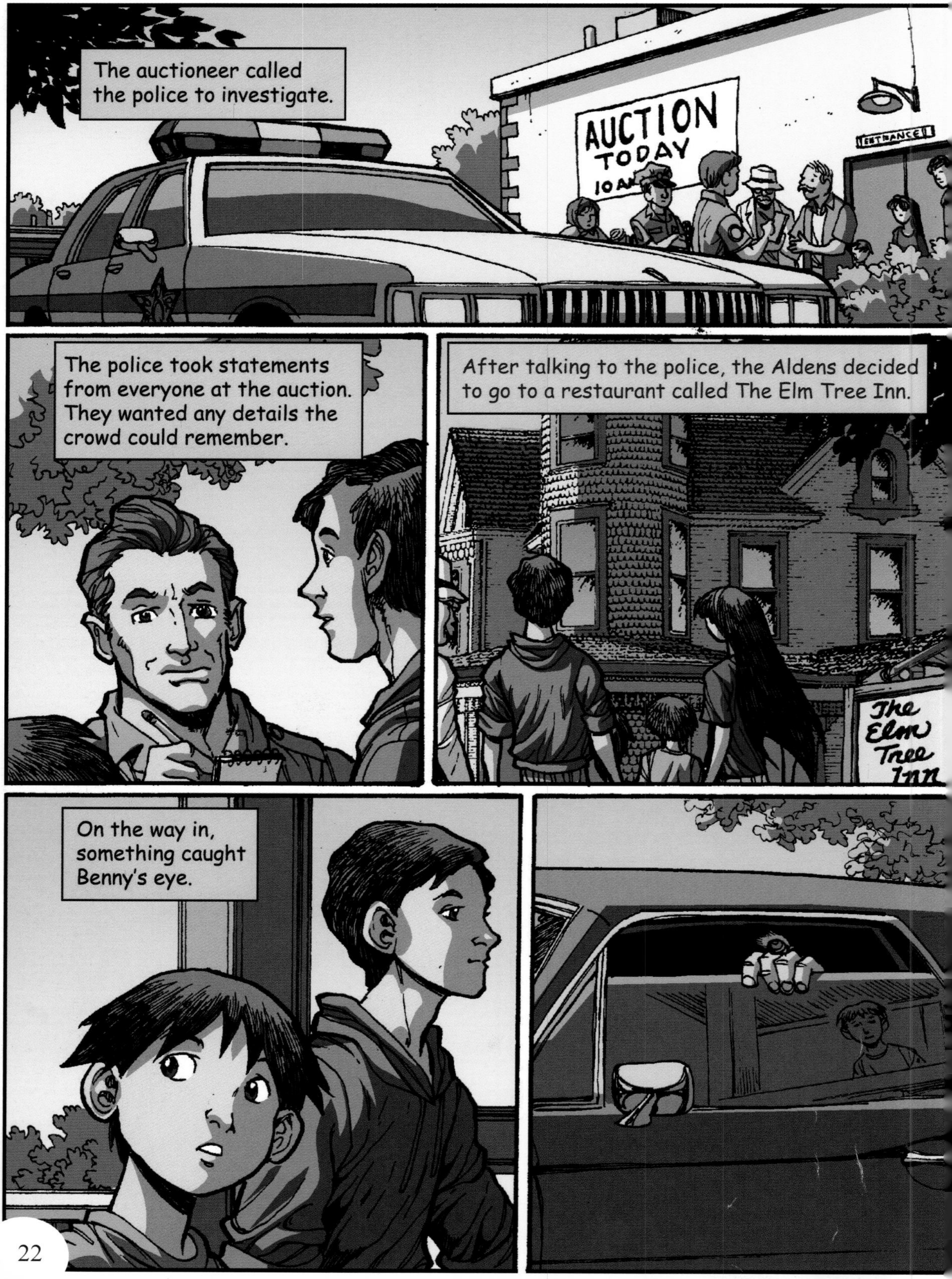

The auctioneer called the police to investigate.
AUCTION TODAY
ENTRANCE
The police took statements from everyone at the auction. They wanted any details the crowd could remember.
After talking to the police, the Aldens decided to go to a restaurant called The Elm Tree Inn.
The Elm Tree Inn
On the way in, something caught Benny's eye.

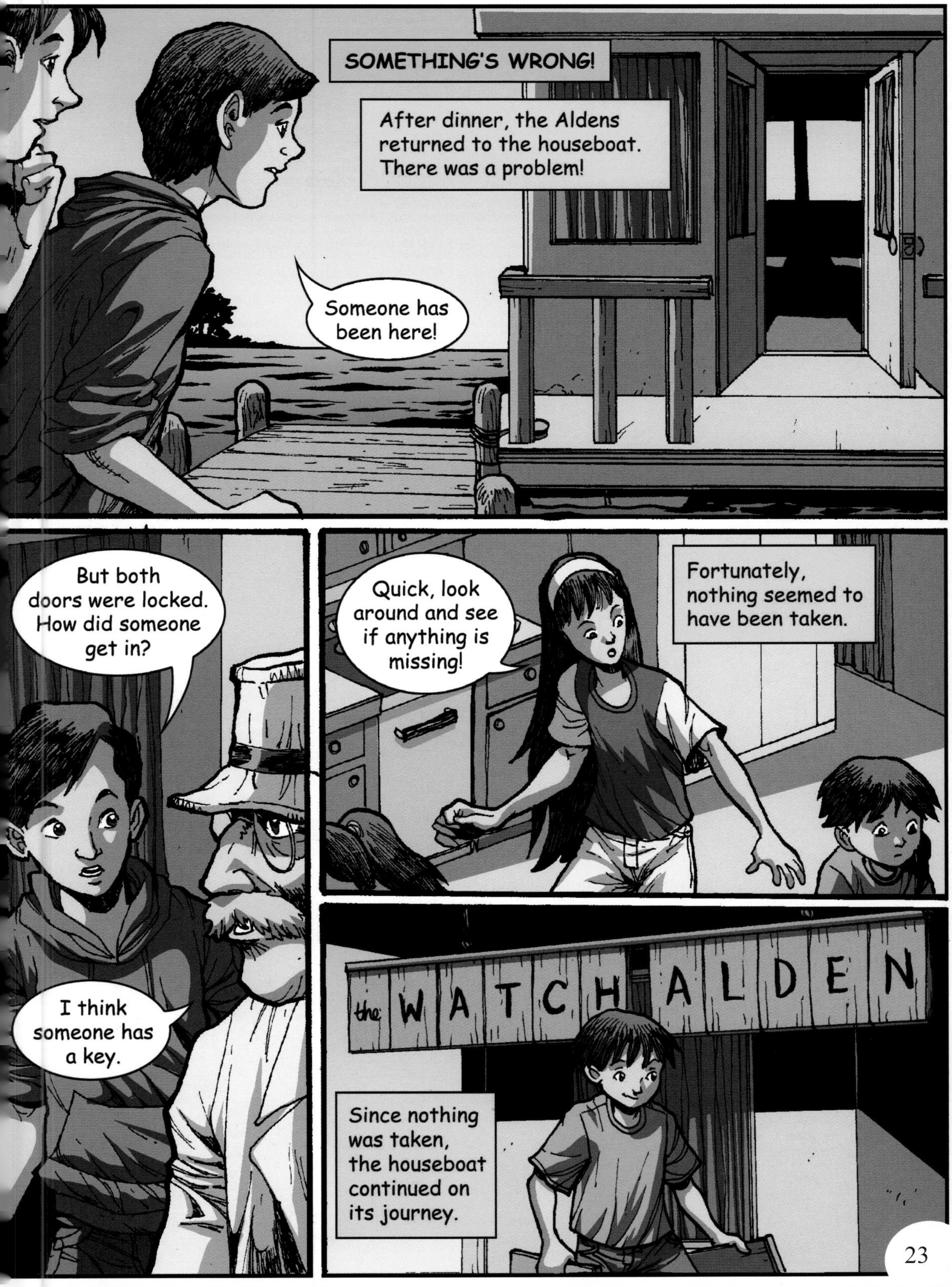
SOMETHING'S WRONG!
After dinner, the Aldens returned to the houseboat. There was a problem!
Someone has been here!
But both doors were locked. How did someone get in?
I think someone has a key.
Quick, look around and see if anything is missing!
Fortunately, nothing seemed to have been taken.
the WATCH ALDEN
Since nothing was taken, the houseboat continued on its journey.

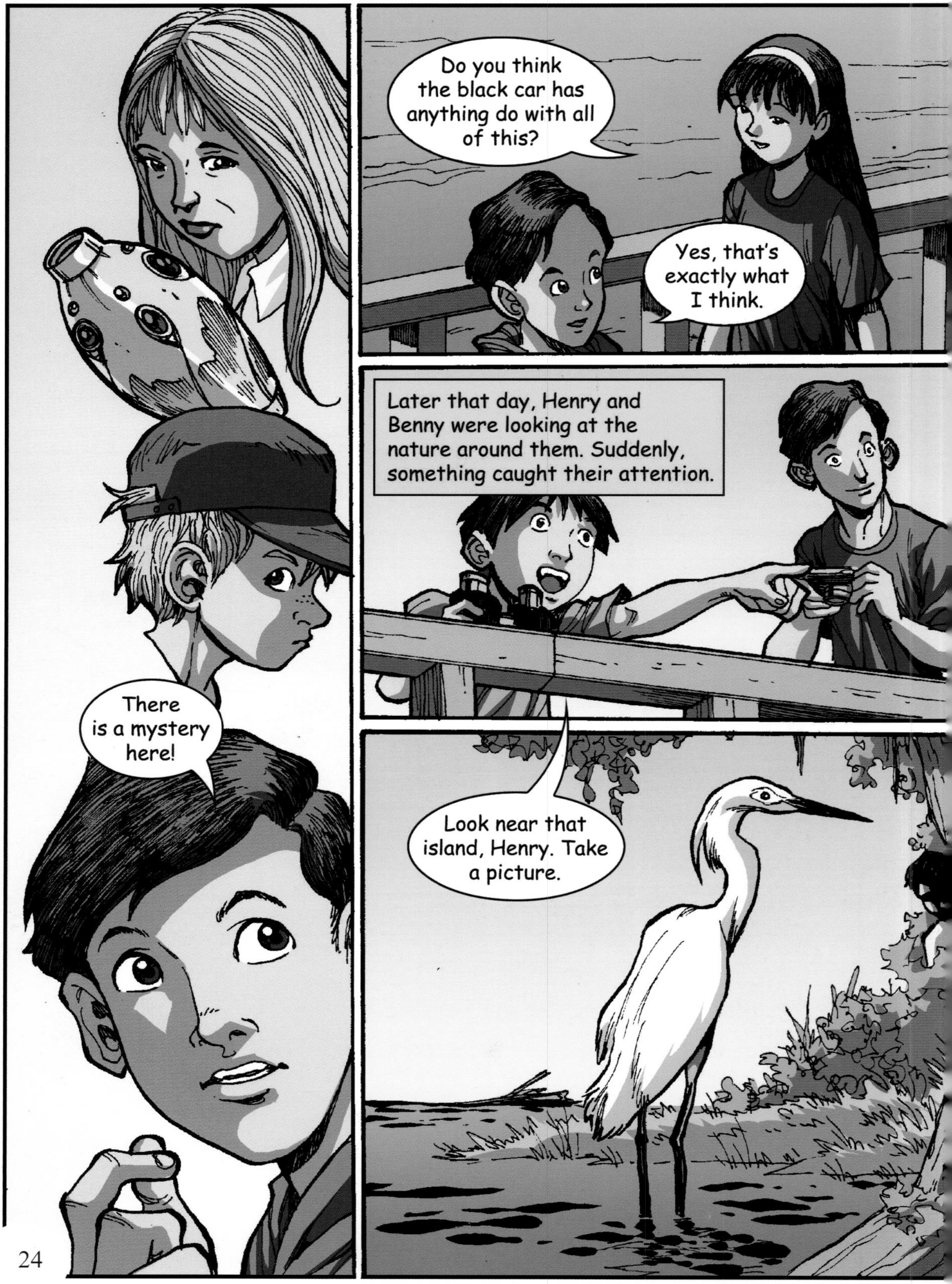
There is a mystery here!
Do you think the black car has anything do with all of this?
Yes, that's exactly what I think.
Later that day, Henry and Benny were looking at the nature around them. Suddenly, something caught their attention.
Look near that island, Henry. Take a picture.

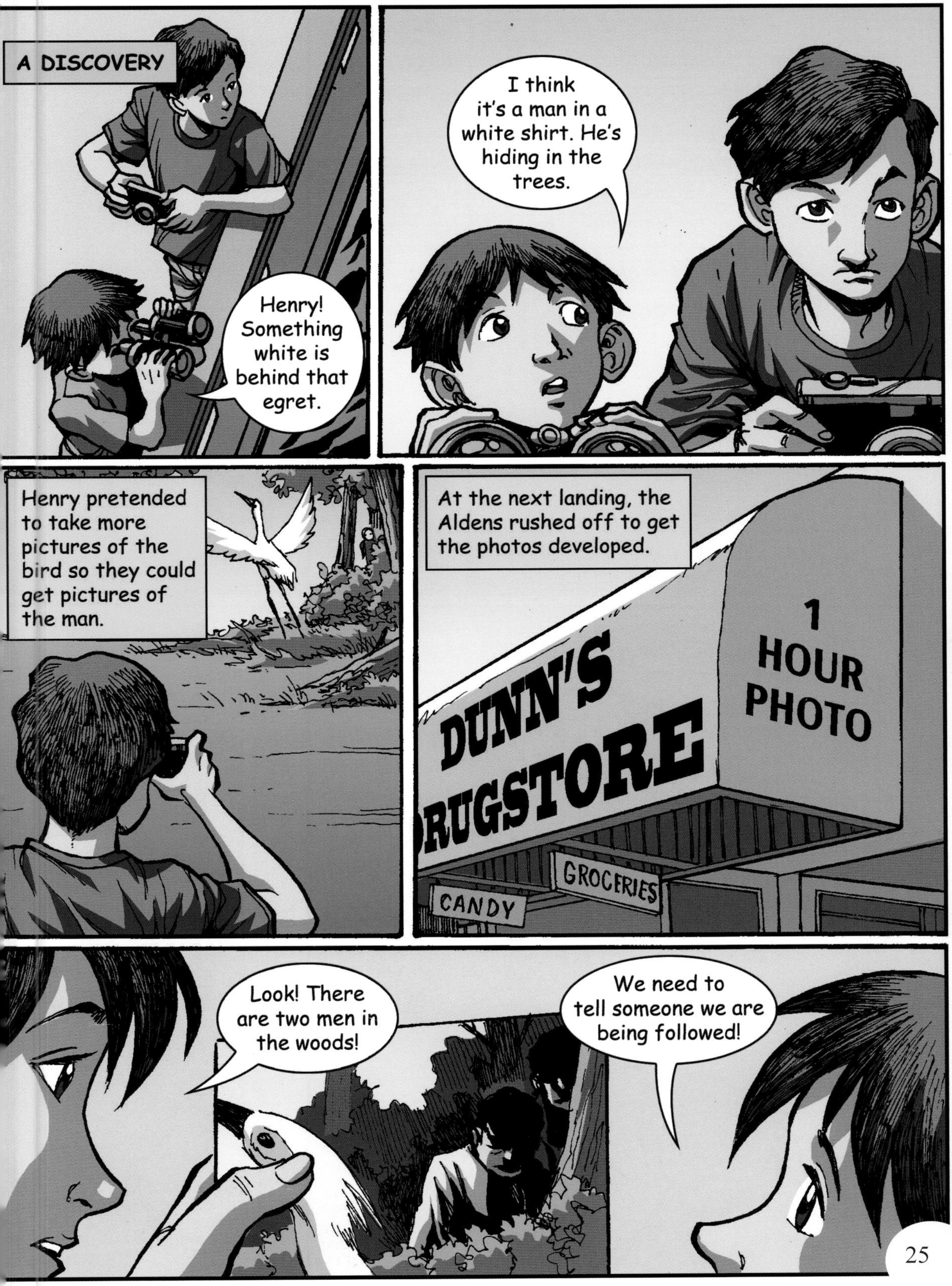
A DISCOVERY
Henry! Something white is behind that egret.
I think it's a man in a white shirt. He's hiding in the trees.
Henry pretended to take more pictures of the bird so they could get pictures of the man.
At the next landing, the Aldens rushed off to get the photos developed.
DUNN'S
RUGSTORE
1 HOUR PHOTO
GROCERIES
CANDY
Look! There are two men in the woods!
We need to tell someone we are being followed!

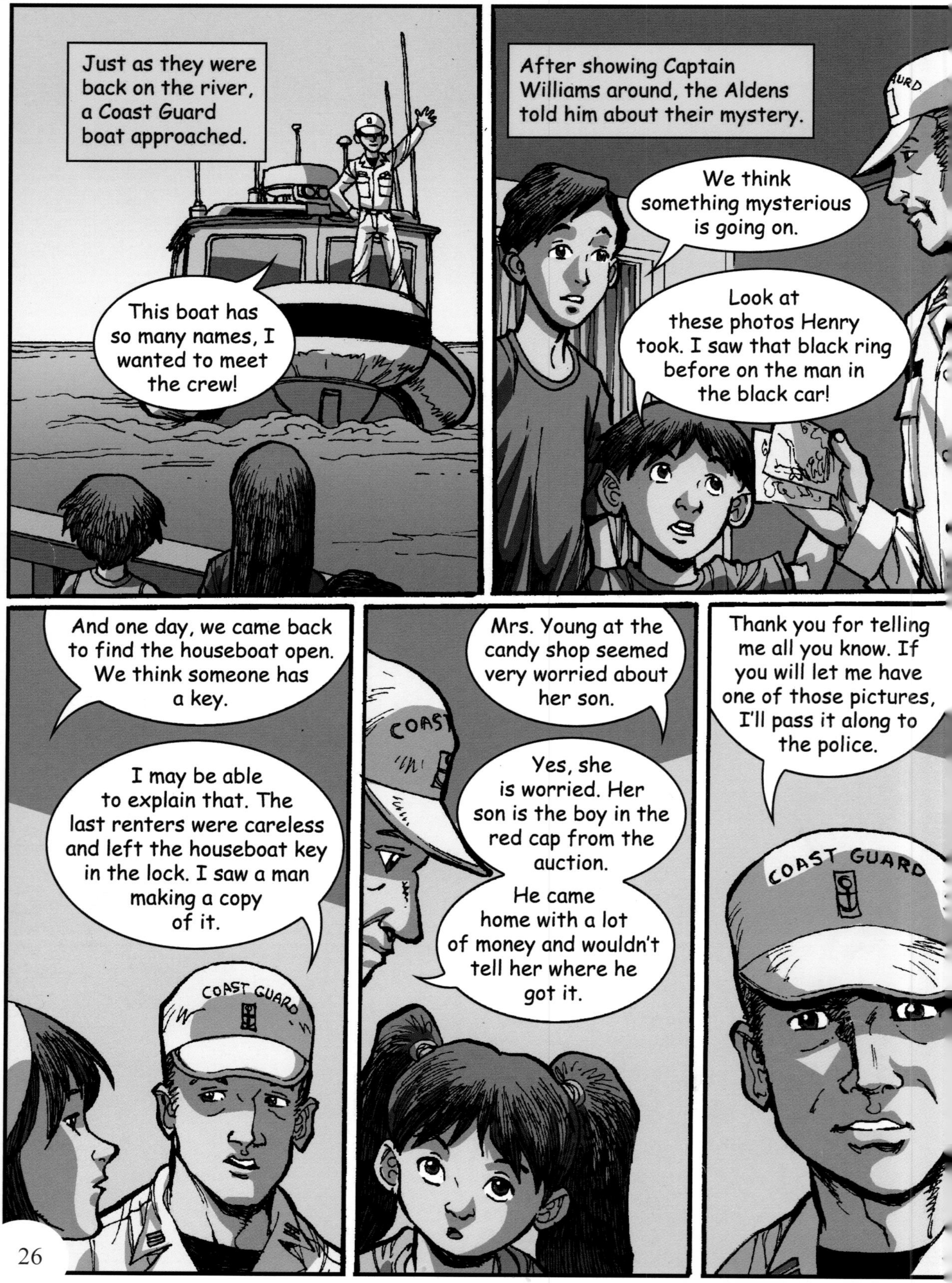
Just as they were back on the river, a Coast Guard boat approached.
This boat has so many names, I wanted to meet the crew!
After showing Captain Williams around, the Aldens told him about their mystery.
We think something mysterious is going on.
Look at these photos Henry took. I saw that black ring before on the man in the black car!
And one day, we came back to find the houseboat open. We think someone has a key.
I may be able to explain that. The last renters were careless and left the houseboat key in the lock. I saw a man making a copy of it.
Mrs. Young at the candy shop seemed very worried about her son.
Yes, she is worried. Her son is the boy in the red cap from the auction.
He came home with a lot of money and wouldn't tell her where he got it.
Thank you for telling me all you know. If you will let me have one of those pictures, I'll pass it along to the police.
COAST GUARD

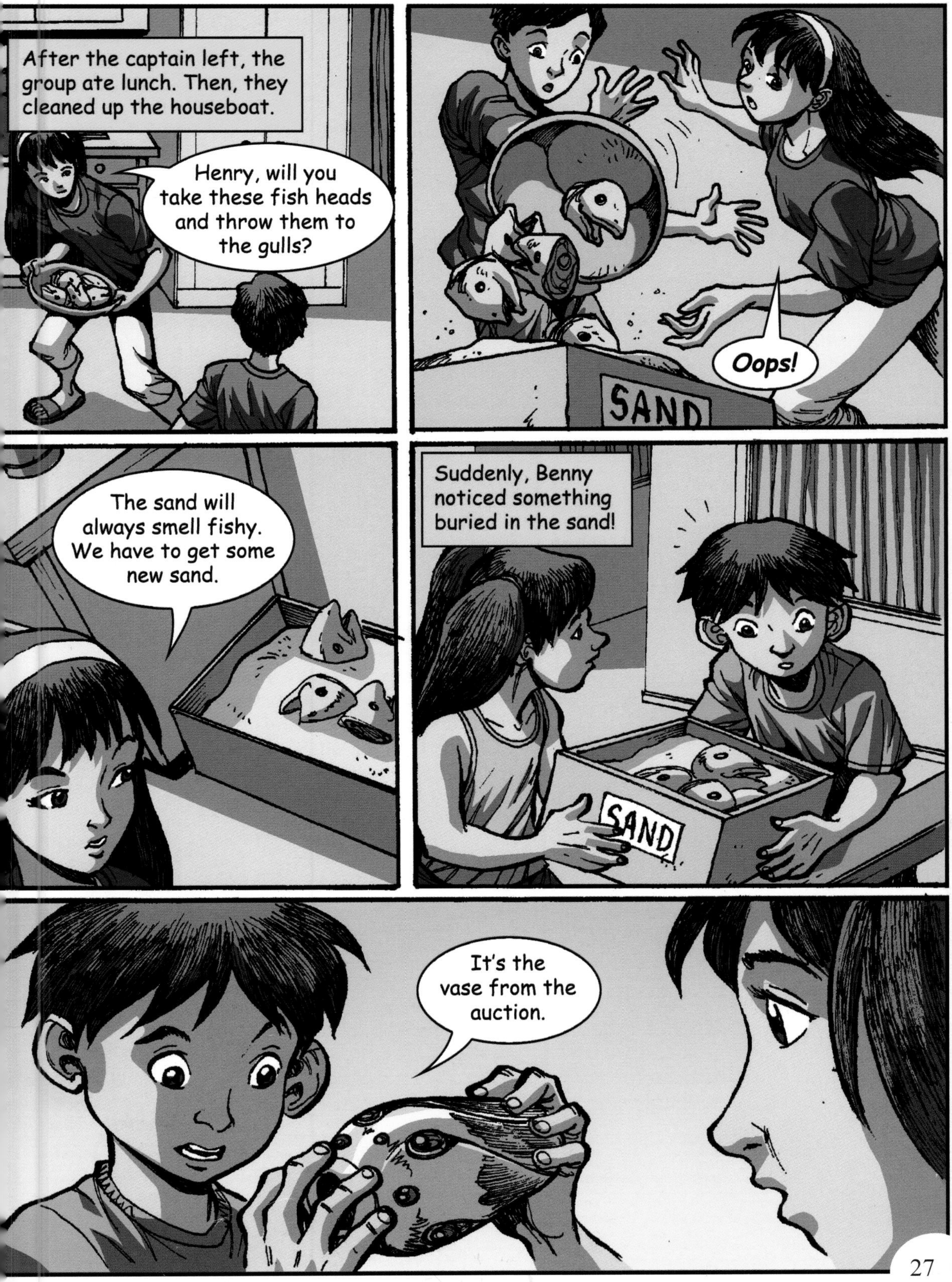
After the captain left, the group ate lunch. Then, they cleaned up the houseboat.
Henry, will you take these fish heads and throw them to the gulls?
Oops!
SAND
The sand will always smell fishy. We have to get some new sand.
Suddenly, Benny noticed something buried in the sand!
SAND
It's the vase from the auction.

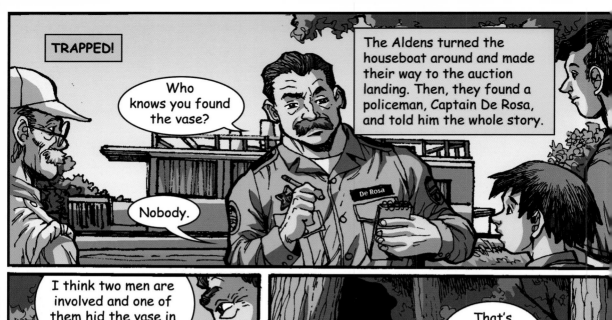

TRAPPED!

Who knows you found the vase?

Nobody.

The Aldens turned the houseboat around and made their way to the auction landing. Then, they found a policeman, Captain De Rosa, and told him the whole story.

I think two men are involved and one of them hid the vase in the box of old clothes.

Then they hired the boy to buy the box and give it to them.

They had to hide the vase somewhere, and your houseboat was just the place.

That's why the man was following us.

We could trap them. We'll just let everybody in town know that we are going to spend the evening on land. Then, the men will go to the houseboat and try to get the vase back.

When they get aboard, you can be in the cabin to catch them.

So the Aldens went to dinner and a movie, letting everyone in town know where they were going to spend the evening.

That's quite a plan.

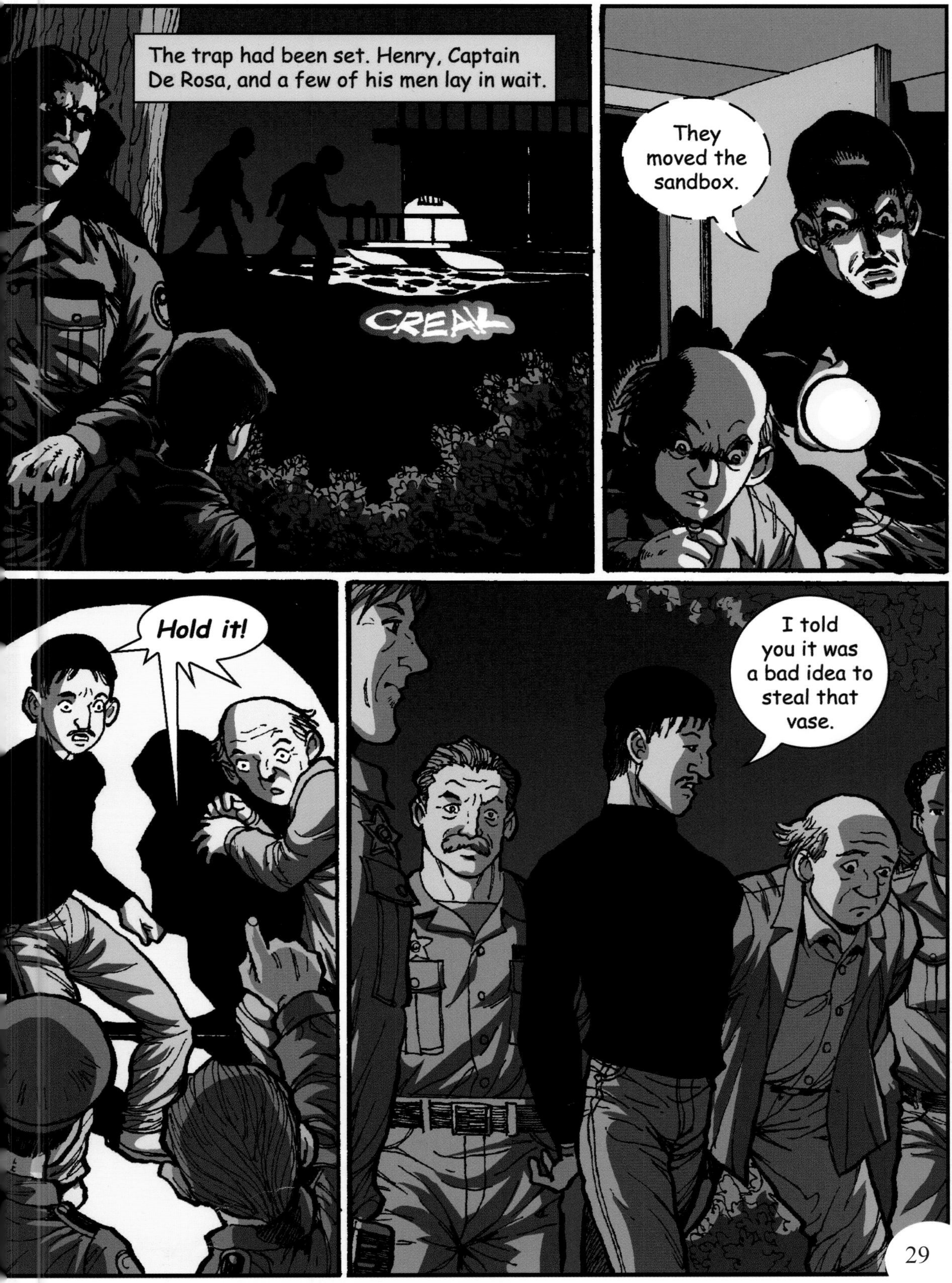

The trap had been set. Henry, Captain De Rosa, and a few of his men lay in wait.
CREAK
They moved the sandbox.
Hold it!
I told you it was a bad idea to steal that vase.

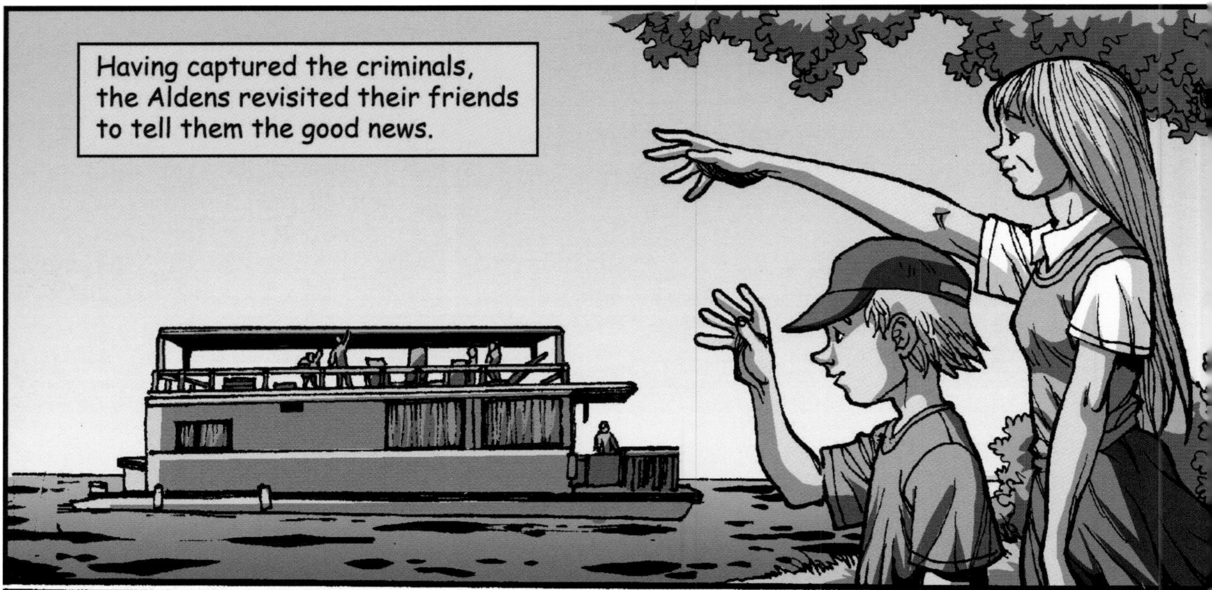
Having captured the criminals, the Aldens revisited their friends to tell them the good news.

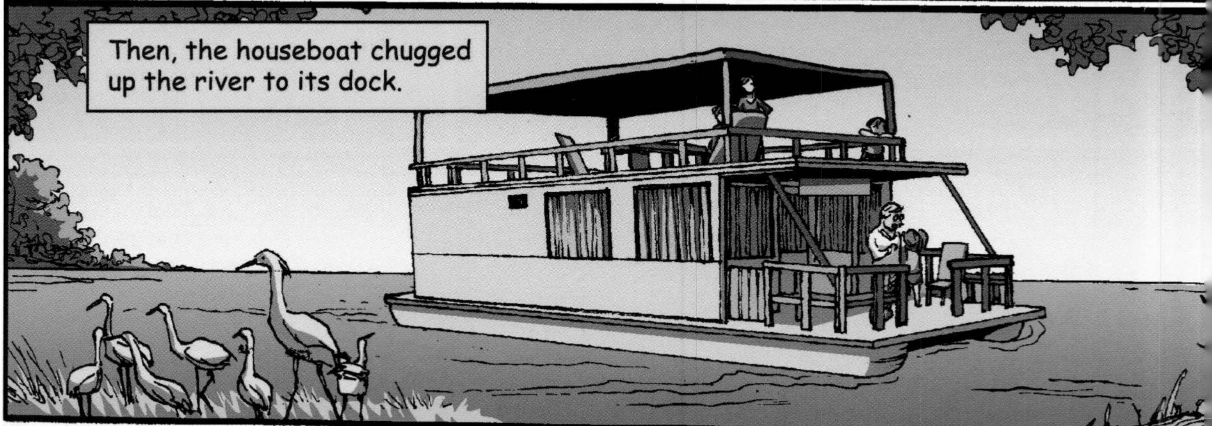
Then, the houseboat chugged up the river to its dock.

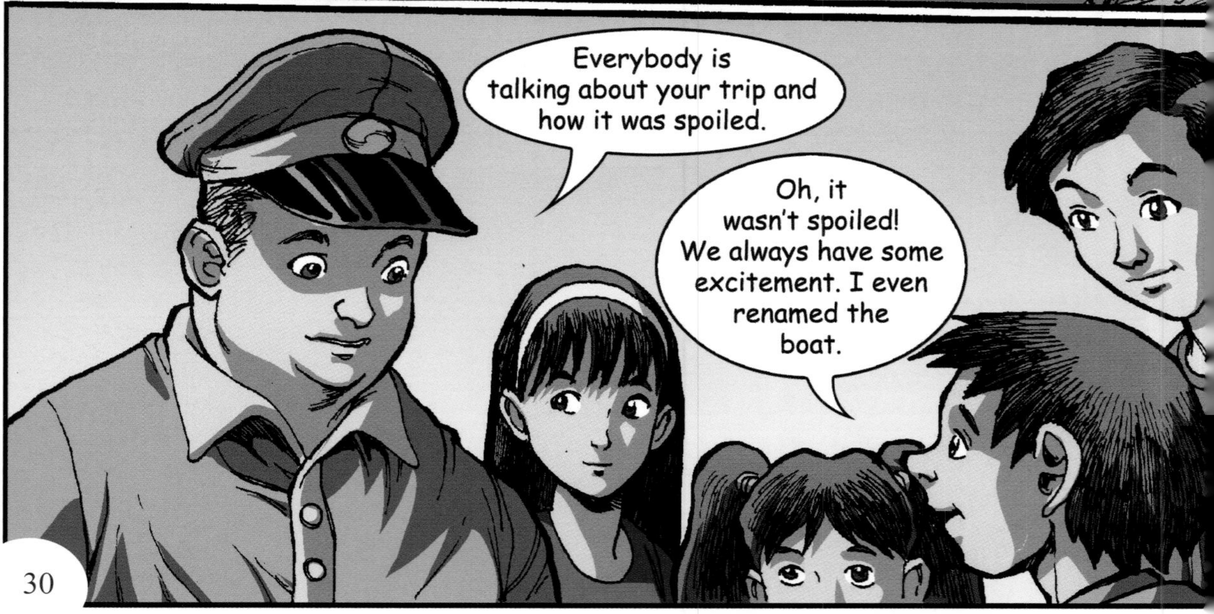
Everybody is talking about your trip and how it was spoiled.
Oh, it wasn't spoiled! We always have some excitement. I even renamed the boat.

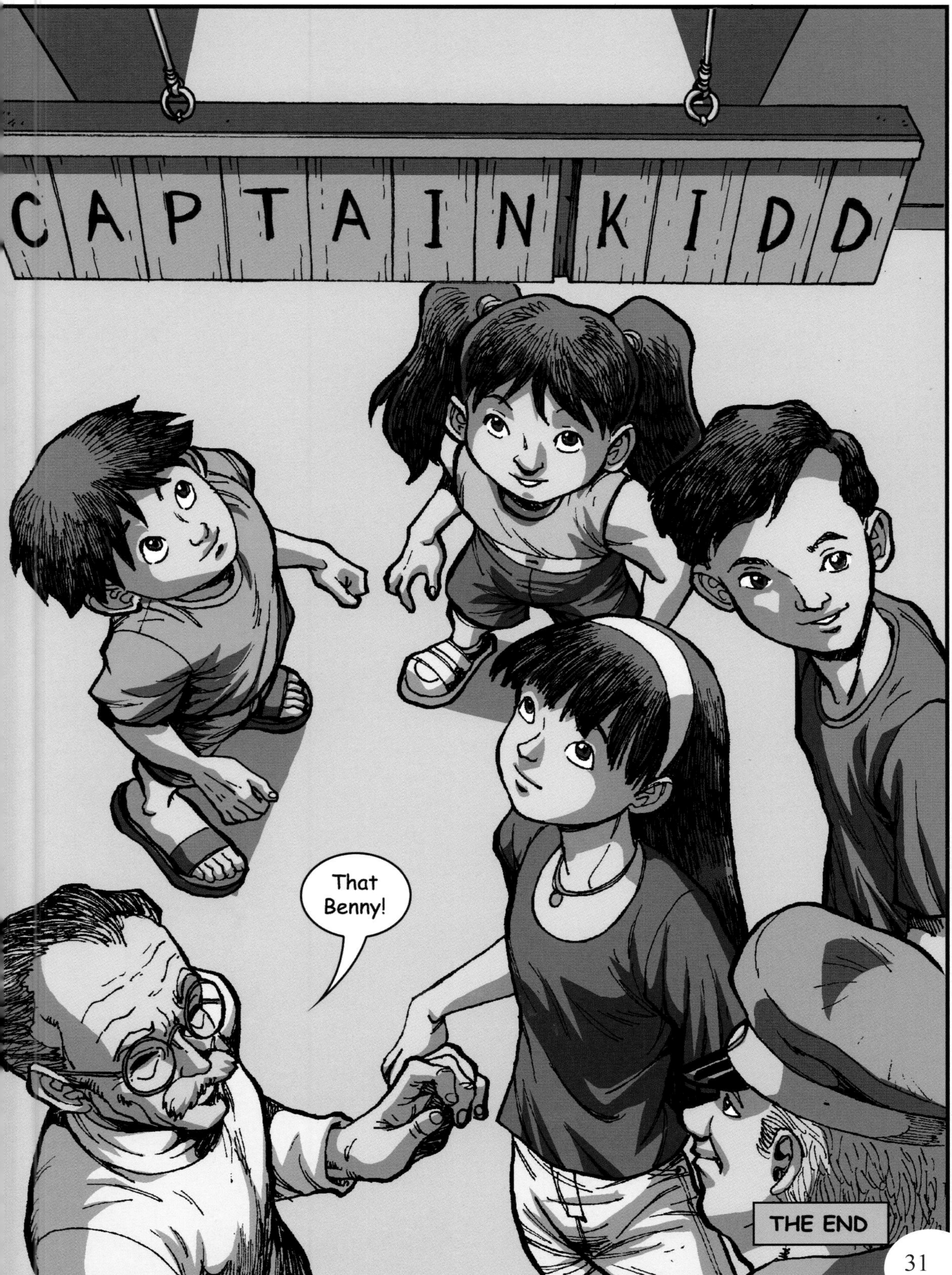
CAPTAIN KIDD
That Benny!
THE END

ABOUT THE CREATOR

Gertrude Chandler Warner was born on April 16, 1890, in Putnam, Connecticut. In 1918, Warner began teaching at Israel Putnam School. As a teacher, she discovered that many readers who liked an exciting story could not find books that were both easy and fun to read. She decided to try to meet this need. In 1942, *The Boxcar Children* was published for these readers.

Warner drew on her own experience to write *The Boxcar Children*. As a child she spent hours watching trains go by on the tracks near her family home. She often dreamed about what it would be like to live in a caboose or freight car—just as the Alden children do.

When readers asked for more Alden adventures, Warner began additional stories. While the mystery element is central to each of the books, she never thought of them as strictly juvenile mysteries. She liked to stress the Aldens' independence. Henry, Jessie, Violet, and Benny go about most of their adventures with as little adult supervision as possible—something that delights young readers.

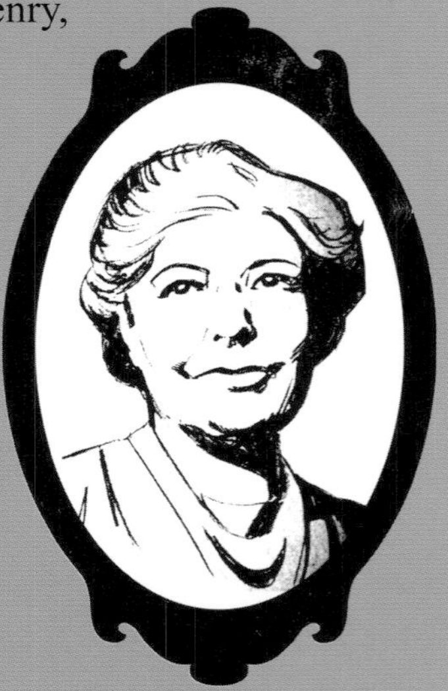

During her lifetime, Warner received hundreds of letters from fans as she continued the Aldens' adventures, writing nineteen Boxcar Children books in all. After her death in 1979, her publisher, Albert Whitman and Company, carried on Warner's vision. Today, the Boxcar Children series has more than 100 books.